"Melissa, don't go."

His voice was velvety soft, making her forget promises she'd made herself, promises that had lost their urgency now. He caressed her cheek with his hand, cupping her chin and tilting it upward, his tantalizing lips waiting only inches from her own.

She braced herself, calling on every ounce of courage she possessed, and pulled away. She could deal with fact, but not with romantic fantasies.

Nothing she knew to be true about Brett Samson meshed with anything she'd heard about him. He'd been tender with her, not threatening. And it was clear he was in over his head.

But that didn't change anything. The gun lay a few feet away, just inside the pocket of his jacket. Did she dare take the chance and disarm the man who held her captive?

W9-DIH-264

Dear Reader,

Be prepared to meet a "Woman of Mystery"!

This month, we're proud to bring you another book in our ongoing Woman of Mystery program, designed to bring you the debut books of writers new to Harlequin Intrigue.

Meet Joanna Wayne, author of *Deep in the Bayou.*

Joanna has always been interested in the risky side of love. Her inspiration for this story came from the idea of being wildly attracted to someone who could also be dangerous, no matter how much you wanted to believe his innocence. Her family felt that way when her husband of ten years whisked her off from a small town in Louisiana to the big, bad city of New Orleans. She's happy to report she's been safe in love ever since!

We're dedicated to bringing you the best new authors, the freshest new voices. Be on the lookout for more Woman of Mystery titles.

Sincerely,

Debra Matteucci
Senior Editor & Editorial Coordinator
Harlequin Books
300 East 42nd Street, Sixth Floor
New York, NY 10017

Deep in the Bayou

Joanna Wayne

Harlequin Books

TORONTO • NEW YORK • LONDON
AMSTERDAM • PARIS • SYDNEY • HAMBURG
STOCKHOLM • ATHENS • TOKYO • MILAN
MADRID • WARSAW • BUDAPEST • AUCKLAND

To my husband for his love and encouragement.
To Linda and Gloria for making me keep working.
And a special thanks to Dr. David Cavanaugh for his
medical expertise.

ISBN 0-373-22288-2

DEEP IN THE BAYOU

Copyright © 1994 by Jo Ann Vest

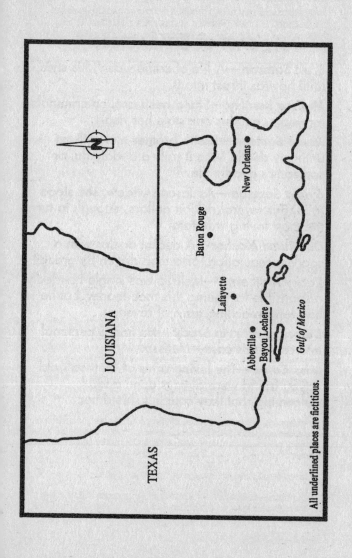

TEXAS

LOUISIANA

Abbeville ●
Bayou Lechere

Lafayette ●

Baton Rouge ●

New Orleans ●

Gulf of Mexico

All underlined places are fictitious.

CAST OF CHARACTERS

Brett Samson—A life of crime wasn't his style, until he was thrust into it.

Melissa Bentley—She'd been around criminals for years, but this one stole her heart.

Jason Samson—Brett's brother met with an untimely death. Was it truly a deadly flu, or someone's deadly plan?

Sylvia Samson—As Jason's widow, she stood to inherit several million dollars, enough to turn the most loving wife fatal.

Dr. Stuart Mosher—A decent doctor with a spotless reputation, or a man driven by greed?

Rocky Matherne—Melissa was single-handedly responsible for jailing this mob leader, but he had long-reaching arms of revenge.

Detective Marvin Brady—He had a personal interest in this case—Melissa.

Miss Cotile—The loving arms of Melissa's old bayou friend were always open and welcoming, but they couldn't shield her.

Prologue

Brett Samson wakened to the sound of a scream. It was a woman's cry, loud and drenched in agony. He opened his eyes, then rubbed persistently to clear them and the confusion that clouded his mind.

For a moment he was back in Wyoming wrapped in a blanket of brilliant stars, and the scream had been only a wild animal announcing its presence and its right to live free.

Slowly the bars on the window above his narrow bed came into focus, and every vestige of the Wyoming dream vanished. Brett traced the lines in his brow with shaking fingers. He had to think, had to fight the drugs that robbed him of logic and memory.

How long had it been since he was brought here, to this place where time had no meaning? It must have been weeks. It was October when he'd arrived in Baton Rouge. October twelfth, his brother Jason's thirtieth birthday. The birthday he'd never lived to celebrate.

Brett beat his fist into the pillow and swallowed bitter tears that rose to choke him. The tears were new, too. Like the shaking and the hallucinations, they'd come with the drugs.

He'd fooled them all at first—the doctors who'd nodded their heads and pretended to listen as he tried to answer their endless probing. And he'd fooled the white-clad care givers. He'd taken their pills and slipped the fingers of one hand past his lips while reaching for a cup of water. He'd watched the other patients and mimicked their awkward movements, their empty stares.

But his tricks weren't working now. They no longer offered him the chalky pills. Now their control came from hypodermics. The medication was plunged into his veins on a regular basis during the well-staffed day hours, but the nights were a different story. They'd stay out of your room during the night for as long as they could—until your screams began. Until your anguish threatened to wake other patients, creating an avalanche of activity for the night crew to handle.

The wee hours of the morning had become Brett's salvation. It was the only time his brain could function with any semblance of clarity. The only time he could plan his escape.

The keys were the answer. The keys swung from the hips of brawny orderlies and jingled in the pockets of unsmiling nurses. They opened drug cabinets, doors to padded rooms and even the tiny cubicles where telephones to the outside world gleamed seductively.

The key he needed was the one that opened the heavy wooden door to the meticulously landscaped courtyard. He knew the key. He'd figured it out while his tricks were still working, while he could still reason and think with measured accuracy. He'd watched the staff go in and out. Watched while young women in business suits led visitors around the wards showing off their "civilized way of handling those with emotional impairments."

And he'd watched while his brother's murderer had walked through the wooden door, her face plastered with makeup and a fake smile, her movements accompanied by the swish of silk and the drumming of her stiletto heels on the polished tiles.

She'd missed her calling. She could've walked away with an Academy Award for her superb performance as bereaved widow and caring sister-in-law. She'd fooled everyone. Almost everyone.

She wasn't going to get off scot-free. Brett would see to that.

But first he had to have the key.

He moaned carefully. It had to be loud enough to fetch the night nurse, soft enough not to frighten her into enlisting the aid of the male orderly.

A sliver of light appeared as his door creaked open.

"What is it, Brett? Do you need something to help you sleep?"

"No, it's just a cramp…in my leg." He stumbled over his words. He had to be just another drugged patient making a routine complaint. He tightened his muscles as she approached the bed.

The jingle of keys in her pocket sharpened his senses. Nurse Sands's fingers closed around his calves. "You're awfully tense, Brett. I'll get something to help you relax."

"No, please, don't go yet." He forced the anxiety from his voice. "Just stay a minute and talk to me. I need to hear the sound of a friendly voice. It's so lonely in here."

Too bad he had to do it this way. Nurse Sands was one of the nice ones.

She moved closer.

Brett said a silent prayer for luck. The keys jingled softly. The time had come.

Chapter One

Melissa Bentley lifted the café mug to her lips and sipped the black coffee. She was tired—tired from the top of her pounding head to the bottoms of her aching feet. The last two weeks had been a dizzying cycle of exhilaration and exhaustion.

The clink of metal sounded across the narrow diner as Melissa watched a burly truck driver yank a copy of the *Times Picayune* from the dispenser. The headlines glared at her from across the room.

Sheriff Linked to Bloody Crime Ring on Election Eve.

Funny, the words seemed detached from her now, as if they hadn't flowed from her own brain just hours earlier. She gulped the remainder of her coffee.

Detached. That's exactly how she felt. Detached from everything except the need for sleep and food. Would it always be this way, she wondered. Is this what cracking the big ones did to you, drained you of every ounce of strength and emotion?

Certainly her first major story had. It had taken two weeks in seclusion on Bayou Lachere before she could even face Robert. He had been her best friend, her lover, her front-page story.

But that had been three years ago. Things were different then. Then her youthful dreams, her naive beliefs in human goodness and happy-ever-after were still unshattered.

An old, familiar ache settled in her stomach. She picked up the stained menu at her elbow. Food couldn't cure this ache, but she hoped it would give her the energy to get a few miles farther down the road.

She longed to soak in a deep tub full of hot water and fragrant bubbles and then sink into a luxuriously soft bed. She would stay there for hours, maybe days, with nothing more disturbing than room service to interrupt her peace. And she wanted it far enough out of New Orleans that no one would recognize her and plague her with questions about the Rocky Matherne story.

She'd done her job. Some other reporter could cover police releases and speculate about the trial. She'd told her editor she'd be on vacation for two weeks. She'd left no phone number and no forwarding address. She deserved a rest.

"What can I get you, honey?"

Melissa glanced at her watch. Ten-thirty. "Are you still serving breakfast?"

"Sure thing. If we got it, you can have it, around the clock."

The words on the menu swam together. Melissa blinked and wiped her weary eyes. "Just toast... and more coffee."

"It's none of my business, honey, but you look like you've had a rough night. Why don't you let me get Butch to cook you up some ham and eggs? Maybe even throw in some of his famous grits and red-eye gravy with a homemade biscuit or two. It's doin' wonders for that fellow over there."

The waitress cocked her head toward a man sitting several booths away. "He looked 'bout as harried as you. Maybe more so."

"Okay, I'll have that."

"The number one breakfast?"

"Whatever you said. That biscuit thing." Melissa didn't have the energy to argue with a well-meaning waitress. "And more coffee, as soon as you can get to it."

"Sure thing, honey. Coming right up."

Melissa leaned back against the padded seat and directed her gaze at the man across the room. God, she hoped she didn't look that bad. His eyes had a wild, almost frightened look. And his hands shook so that he could barely get the fork to his lips.

Sad, Melissa thought, another life lost to drugs or booze, or... She closed her eyes.

"You all right?"

The strident voice of the waitress startled Melissa, and she jerked awake, her eyes staring at a food-spattered name tag that provided the voice with an identity.

"You let that second cup of coffee get plumb cold."

"I'm fine, Nina. Guess I just dozed off for a minute."

"Yeah, I guess you did," she answered, a trace of pity in her voice. "Food's almost ready. I'll pour this out and get you some hot."

Struggling to keep her eyes open, Melissa watched the guy across the room dunk a huge biscuit into his gravy and then pop half of it into his mouth. He was shaking less now and attacking his food with a vengeance.

He didn't look much older than she was, probably somewhere around thirty, and strangely enough, he had a rugged attraction about him. His tanned, muscular body was a vivid contradiction to his pathetic shaking.

But then, who was she to talk? Thirty-six hours without sleep and an oversize sweat suit wouldn't win her any beauty contests, either.

Nor was it providing total anonymity. The stranger's gaze was focused on her now, and her skin seemed to crawl beneath his scrutiny. Defying her own uneasiness, she returned his stare, but he didn't look away. Not until his hand began to shake and his fork fell from his fingers to the wooden floor.

A curse flew from his lips.

"Hate to be in his shoes." Nina voiced her opinion loudly as she slapped an overflowing plate in front of Melissa. She poured another cup of coffee, letting some of it slosh from the cup onto the table. Taking a corner of her apron, she wiped it away. "Eat up, honey."

"I will. It must be good, judging from the way our friend over there was going at it."

"Yeah. No table manners, that guy."

"Is he a regular customer?" Melissa couldn't curb her curiosity.

"Never seen him before. Tried to talk to him, but he ain't a bit sociable. It's no wonder Carl's dumping him off here."

"Dumping him off?"

"Yeah. Carl said he picked him up outside New Orleans. He knows he shouldn't be picking up hitchhikers, company policy being what it is. But he gets lonesome driving by himself all the time. That's Carl over there," she volunteered, motioning toward the burly truck driver, almost hidden by his newspaper. "And he's sure big enough to take care of himself."

"I wonder why Carl doesn't care for the man's company?" Melissa baited.

"Like I said, the man don't talk. Don't listen, either. Carl said he just stared off into space or rubbed his forehead like he was trying to work out something in his own mind. He's in some kinda trouble." Nina nodded her head knowingly.

"Is that your assessment, or Carl's?"

"Carl said it first, but I would've known it anyway. We get all kinds in here. All kinds. Now you just eat up, honey, before your food gets cold. Just keep your distance from the likes of him."

"I plan to." At least for the next few weeks, Melissa assured herself, as she bit into one of the flaky biscuits. She'd keep her distance from even the smell of trouble.

She savored the taste of the peppery eggs and then cut into the thick slice of hickory-smoked ham. Nina was right. Food was just what she needed, and it didn't get much better than this.

Melissa quickly finished off the eggs and most of the grits. It hadn't taken the unfriendly stranger long, either. By the time she'd eased her hunger pains, he'd dropped a few crumpled bills on the table and disappeared.

Nina was probably right about him, too. He was likely in some kind of trouble, and Melissa couldn't help but speculate as to what it might be. Whatever it was, he was trying to get out of New Orleans. And whoever Carl was, he was a brave man to pick up someone like that. Brave or crazy.

Melissa paid her bill and stepped outside. The wind had picked up, and dark clouds that had threatened thunderstorms all day were on the verge of keeping their promise. She was thankful she'd filled her gas tank earlier.

A flash of lightening zigzagged across the sky, chased by a booming crash of thunder. Head down, she pulled her raincoat around her tightly and scurried toward her car. She'd drive a few more miles, over into Texas, and then stop at the first decent motel. Luxury was less important now. Any bed would do.

Jerking the car door open, she flung herself behind the wheel as the first drops of rain pelted savagely against the windshield. But her sigh of relief was lost, muffled by the scream that began deep in her throat.

A strong hand covered her mouth, and a cold cylinder bore into her ribs.

"Drive."

Chapter Two

Melissa's breath came in painful gasps. She opened her mouth to scream, but no sound came, none but the hammering of her heart racing out of control. She had to think, to stop the paralyzing panic, but she could only stare in silence at the figure beside her.

It was him. The man from the diner. Still shaking, but undoubtedly holding the upper hand.

"Drive," he repeated, his voice low but demanding. "Don't make me do something we'll both regret."

She slipped the key into the ignition and lowered the gearshift into Reverse. Breathing deeply, she forced a calm into her voice. "Where?"

"West. Just drive west on I-10 until I tell you to do differently. Don't try anything foolish."

Melissa did as she was told. The pistol in her ribs was a powerful incentive not to try anything, foolish or otherwise. At five foot four and one hundred and fifteen pounds, she wouldn't pose much of a threat. Not to a gun-wielding man at least six feet tall and solid muscle.

But brawn was no match for brains. She just had to clear her mind, size up the situation, figure out what made this man tick.

Rocky! That was it. He had to be the mastermind behind this. She'd brought his bloody reign to an end, and this was her payback. His one last act of vengeance.

The performance in the diner was all a ruse. Witnesses would describe a shaking, drugged hitchhiker who was there when she was last seen. They would believe she was his chance victim. In the wrong place at the wrong time.

Somehow she had to convince him that Rocky couldn't control him anymore. He couldn't control anyone now, unless he could do it from a jail cell.

"How long have you worked for Rocky?"

"Rocky?"

"Rocky Matherne. This trick isn't going to fool anyone. Rocky's on his way to prison, and he'll be there for a long time. He can't help you or hurt you now. You'd be wise to forget his orders and just get away from here."

"Lady, I've never been accused of being too wise, but I'm trying my best to get as far away from here as I can. The problem is I keep getting stuck with people who can't stop talking."

"My name's Melissa, not lady." She'd read that somewhere. Make sure the abductor knows your name. Make them realize you're a real person. Of course, if he was working for Rocky, he probably already knew her name and a whole lot more.

She knew nothing about him. Absolutely nothing, and she'd been in enough dangerous situations to know that what you didn't know *could* hurt you.

Her chances of getting out of this mess alive would be a whole lot better if she could study him closely, but it was impossible to take her eyes from the road for longer than an instant. The rain was falling steadily, and visibility was no more than a few yards.

She'd have to get him to talk. "Are you in some kind of trouble?"

"No. No trouble. I just do this sort of thing for a hobby. You know, some men play golf, I kidnap beautiful women."

He had a sense of humor. That was a good sign, even if the humor was a bit caustic. It humanized him a little. Now to keep him talking. "That was a stupid question, I guess."

"Yes, but my guess is you're not a stupid woman. I don't know who Rocky Matherne is, and I don't care, but I can assure you he's not controlling me."

Melissa's hands tightened on the wheel as she swerved to miss a cardboard box that had blown onto the highway. "What does control you?"

"Nothing...usually."

For a moment he studied her intently, then turned and stared out the window. His profile was rugged, defiant. Skin bronzed from years spent in wind and sun showed his virility in spite of the fragility of his emotional state. He probably *was* in control, most of the time, but not now. Today he was following a path of destruction. Hers as well as his.

She straightened her back, girding her strength about her. She couldn't give in to thoughts of destruction. There were ways out of any situation, and she'd find a way out of this. But now was not the time to make her move. The gun was cradled in his lap like a baby, and his fingers caressed the cold steel.

For now there was nothing to do but drive and fight the fear that rose up like poisonous smoke. Drive and think. And pray.

The man beside her finally broke the ominous silence. "Louisiana thunderstorms, I'd almost forgotten their fury." His voice was soft, little more than a murmur, as if he was talking more to himself than to her.

She kept her eyes glued to the road. The rain fell in sheets, and her body ached with tenseness, her fingers from the death grip she held on the wheel. "We have to stop. Driving in this rain is suicide."

Suicide. She shuddered at her choice of words. Death of any kind was not a comforting thought.

"Why don't you let me out... anywhere," she continued. "You take the car. Drive on over into Texas and just keep going."

"Keep going? Sure. Keep going until the cops you call stop me about five miles down the road. Look, lady..."

"Melissa."

He glared at her, almost daring her to say more. "Believe me, there's nothing I'd like better than to do this solo. But I can't. Not yet."

"What if I give you my word that I won't call the police?"

"I wouldn't believe you. Trust is not a luxury I can afford right now. I need you for a while longer. Just try to relax. And stop talking, so I can think."

"I could relax a lot better if you'd get rid of that gun."

"But *I* couldn't." The slightest trace of a smile crossed his lips. "I'll put it out of sight, though, if that'll make you feel better."

"Thanks."

The shaking was noticeable as he slipped the semiautomatic into the front pocket of his Windbreaker. The tremors seemed to come and go without warning.

She wasn't sure about his association with Rocky, but evidently the drug bit was no ruse.

He stared straight ahead. "I guess you're right . . . about the weather. We'll be crossing the Texas state line in another mile or so. Soon as we do, pull in at the first cheap motel. We'll get a room, rest for a while."

"No!" The word flew from her lips. The last thing she wanted was to go to a motel room with this man. He was no ordinary criminal. Somehow she was sure of that. But abducting females was not the trademark of a gentleman.

His hand touched her arm, and her blood turned to ice water. His fingers were rough on her skin, callused, but his touch was gentle. "I told you, lady, just relax. I've never taken a woman against her will, and I'm not starting now, even if I could, which is doubtful with all the crap they've forced into my body over the last few weeks."

Drugs. That had to be the crap he was talking about. But why would someone be forcing them on him? Unless he was ill, physically . . . or mentally.

"That sounds rough." She tried to keep the rising panic from her voice. "Why would someone do that to you?"

"That's exactly what I intend to find out." He turned toward the window. "The sign said Stop 'N Sleep Motel next exit. We'll try that one. I could use a couple hours of sleep. You could, too."

"I'm not tired, really."

"No? You were a little while ago. You could barely keep your eyes open back at the truck stop."

True, she admitted to herself, but she wasn't now. Adrenaline was a powerful stimulant. Still, the motel might not be such a bad idea. There'd be people there. With a little luck, she'd find a way to signal that she needed help.

She drove the next five miles in silence and then took the exit ramp. The motel was just ahead, but the driveway was buried beneath the rising water. She slowed to a crawl.

"Pull in here." He grabbed the wheel, swerving the car to the right.

Melissa eased through half a foot of water and then over a small hill. She breathed a sigh of relief. At least a dozen cars were in the parking lot. Usually a place like this would be deserted this time of day, but evidently the rain had sent others scurrying for shelter, too.

Great. The more people there were around, the better her chances were at recruiting help.

"Talk about cheap. Not even a covered entrance. We'll get soaked getting out in this."

"No use for both of us to drown," she answered. "Besides, I have a raincoat. Why don't you stay in the car and I'll go in and register? You can watch everything I do through the window. I'm not crazy enough to try anything."

Afraid of his reaction, Melissa kept her head lowered. Surely he could see through her offer, but she had to take that chance. He was on drugs, and a man on drugs didn't think too clearly.

"You never give up, do you, lady?"

"No, and I could help you, if you'd let me. I know a lot of people."

"I'll just bet you do. What kind of help are you planning to get me?"

"I don't know. How can I unless you tell me what's going on?"

"Right now you only need to know one thing. We're Mr. and Mrs. Bill Jones. And remember, when we get inside, I'll do all the talking, though I know that's hard for you."

"And if I don't remember, then what? You don't seem the type to shoot me or anyone else." She held her breath. She was bluffing, and she was playing against a stacked deck.

He slipped his hand into the pocket that held the gun. "Don't make us find out."

HE TURNED THE KEY and pushed open the heavy door. The room was dingy, the once-white paint yellowed and peeling. The carpet smelled of spills and mildew and the smoke from countless cigarettes. A double bed with a sagging mattress stood between two small tables, and light from the lamps fell eerily across the faded, flowered spread.

The panic hit again, rising in her throat with suffocating force. Would this nightmare never end?

She'd been so sure she'd have a chance to escape or at least to signal someone. Once inside the motel office, she'd taken a paper towel from the counter and begun to wipe the rain from her face and dripping hair while her eyes and mind had sized up the situation.

Bill Jones, or whoever the heck he was, kept one hand on the gun in his pocket the whole time he inquired about a room. The other hand had rested possessively around Melissa's waist. Worse, a young boy, apparently the manager's kid, had sat on the floor behind the desk, marching plastic dinosaurs around in circles.

She'd had no choice but to play her abductor's game, not daring to do anything to make him lose control. A man in his condition might just start shooting at any-one and anything in his path. There had been nothing she could do but go along—until the time was right. But she'd get her chance. After all, she was the one with her wits about her. He was the one coming off a major overdose.

He took her arm and pulled her inside. "Whew! Place smells worse than a garbage dump. We'd have probably been better off sleeping in the car."

Melissa watched while he locked the door with the key and then slipped the key into his jeans pocket.

Drat. The motel was old, too old. The doors hadn't been updated to meet the new fire safety standards. They locked from the inside and outside with a key. This was going to be a challenge, but not impossible. There was still the window.

"Well, at least it's dry." She tried to sound relieved. "And there's a bathroom." She started through the half-open door.

"Wait." He grabbed her arm and held her at his side while he examined the tiny room. "Okay. It looks safe enough. No windows. But leave the door open a crack." He pulled her handbag from her shoulder. "And leave that out here. You never know what you women carry around in those things."

"I don't carry a gun, if that's what you're afraid of. But I will after this." She hurled the words recklessly. Even danger couldn't keep her tongue bound forever. She'd had about enough of this two-bit criminal. "You'll find some money, though. Help yourself, or are you above stealing?"

"Look, lady, I don't want to argue with you, and I don't want your money, although I may need a loan until I can get my hands on some of my own. But right now I'm just trying to buy some time.''

Frustration edged his shaky voice, and he ran his fingers through his damp hair. "Time to think. Time to find some answers. Time to clear my mind from these damn drugs.''

He turned and stared at her with dark, tortured eyes, and she felt as if he was pleading silently for help. Strange, she thought, she was the kidnap victim, yet the man with the gun sounded more confused, more helpless than she'd felt since he'd abducted her. And he was not used to being in such a predicament. Somehow she was sure of that.

She walked into the bathroom shaking her head. This was ridiculous. She was almost feeling sorry for him.

Almost, but not quite.

As soon as she was out of his sight, she searched for any object that might be used as a weapon. There was nothing. Plastic cups and an imitation mirror that wasn't even glass. She swallowed tears and stared at the yellowed fixtures, searching her memory for clues as to who this man might be and what he wanted from her.

It could, of course, be just as it appeared. A quirk of fate that had thrown her into the path of an emotionally distraught man. The worst kind of emotionally distraught man. One with a gun.

Or she could be the target in a meticulously staged drama of revenge. If not Rocky, then someone else. She had plenty of enemies. There was no doubt about that. Everyone in her line of work did.

Possibilities whirled through her mind until the sound of angry voices from the bedroom yanked her to reality.

"I told you. I'm innocent. My arrest is all Melissa Bentley's doing. But she'll pay for her ruthless lies. Mark my words. Hers is coming to her, and it won't be pretty."

Melissa's heart slammed against her chest. Rocky. There was no mistaking the harsh tone and ninth-ward accent.

"But Rocky Matherne remains behind bars tonight..."

The TV. It was only the TV. Her breathing returned to near normal, and she pushed open the bathroom door. "Surely you can find something better than that to watch?" she remarked, trying to sound disinterested.

"No," he answered, flicking off the set. "It's on every channel." He studied her carefully, and she backed away, turning her face from his.

"You keep pretty rough company, don't you?" he asked. "What's your connection with Rocky Matherne?"

"What makes you think there is a connection?"

"Why else would you have assumed I was his hit man?"

"I don't know. I'd just heard about his arrest. I guess I jumped to conclusions."

"And now you've changed your mind about that?"

"Yes." Surprisingly, her answer was honest. She knew he was mixed up in something serious, but it was not Rocky's brand of horror. She didn't believe him capable of that, and she prayed her intuition was right this time. "I'm not even sure who this Rocky fellow is."

"You're lying."

"What do you mean?"

"Simply that. There's more to this Rocky Matherne thing than you're admitting. Were you one of his girl-friends?"

"Maybe."

"You're lying again. You may as well tell me the truth." He walked to the window and stared at the pouring rain. "It looks as if we're going to be together for quite a while."

"Okay, I'll tell you the truth if you'll agree to do the same."

"I don't bargain."

Melissa watched as he reached for a glass of water. His hands shook, and the clear liquid spilled over the edges of the glass, pooling on the painted surface of the metal table.

"Damn!" he muttered before lifting the glass to his lips and draining it dry. "If this is what drugs do to you, no wonder the country's falling apart."

"It's what they do in the beginning. It gets worse."

"You sound as if you know. From personal experience?"

"No."

"I didn't think so. You don't look the type. But then, you don't look the Rocky Matherne type, either."

"Well, that's something." She needed to keep him talking even though the conversation seemed to be headed down a dead-end street. But as long as he was talking, her danger was minimized. "What type do you take me for?"

"It's hard to say. You're dressed in sneakers and sweats, but that car of yours didn't come cheap. Neither did that diamond watch you're wearing."

"It's an imitation."

"And you're a terrible liar."

Melissa studied the pattern of stains in the carpet. She didn't like the way he looked at her, scrutinizing, almost seeming to read her mind.

"You're ambitious, though. Or worried. Whatever you've been doing, you've been doing with a passion, obviously not even taking time to sleep."

Melissa shivered. The man was smart. Too smart. Even coming off the drugs. She'd have to stay on her toes every minute to stay ahead of him.

"There's something striking about you," he continued, his voice growing low and gravelly. "It's the eyes, I think. Black as night... and intriguing. The kind of eyes that could get a man into a lot of trouble."

Melissa raked away a damp curl that had fallen over her forehead and pushed her dark, shoulder-length hair behind her ears. Plain and simple. That's how she wanted to look. The plainer the better.

He clinched his hands into fists, and the strong muscles in his arm strained against the cotton fabric of his shirt. "But there's something gentle about you. Too pretty to be tough, but you are. There's no doubt about that. I know this isn't easy for you." His gaze fell to the floor. "But there just isn't any other way."

"Yes, there is."

"Yeah, sure. And if we just believe, Tinker Bell will sprinkle a little fairy dust around, and we'll all fly off to Never Never Land."

"Bitter, aren't you?"

"Yeah, but I'll get over it. When I finish taking care of business."

"What kind of business?"

He sat on the edge of the bed, and the worn springs groaned and sagged beneath his masculine frame. "I plan to see that a certain woman pays for her crime."

"So that's what this is about. Some macho form of revenge."

"Not revenge. Justice."

His words began to slur, and the tremors attacked with renewed vengeance. Melissa knew his fatigue and the effects of the drugs had to be blurring his capabilities. All she had to do was stay awake—and alive—until he made a mistake.

"Then you're in luck," she announced. "Insuring justice is my business."

"Oh, no! Say it isn't so. But it'd be just my luck. On the lam and I kidnap a lady lawyer."

"I'm not a lawyer." Melissa chose her words carefully. "I'm a reporter, an investigative reporter. I search out hidden facts and reveal them to people who can do something about injustices."

He let out a low whistle. "A reporter. Well, isn't this just dandy? No wonder you seem so tough. What's a mere kidnapping to an investigative reporter who smells a story? Hidden facts, family secrets, a little dirt. Who cares? A story's a story."

Melissa's patience stretched ... cracked ... broke. "Now listen here, Mr. Whoever-you-are. I was sitting in a restaurant minding my own business when you decided you needed a ride. I didn't ask for your company. You demanded mine. I don't know what your problem with reporters is, and I don't care. But for your information, I'm not a dirt grubber. I've risked my life more than once to dig up the real facts, and—"

She threw up her hands and sank into the room's one chair. "I don't know why I'm wasting my breath defending myself to a common criminal."

He rose from the bed and walked toward her. His hand shot out in her direction. Melissa jumped from the chair, bracing herself for a blow.

"You do take me for a beast, don't you?" he said, as he reached past her and lifted her handbag from the table. He scavenged through the purse's several compartments until he found what he was looking for.

"Melissa Bentley." He nodded knowingly as he read her name from her press ID card. "So that's your connection with Rocky Matherne."

"Like I told you, I dig up facts that help bring the guilty to justice."

"You're quite a hero, or is it heroine? Grammar was never my strong suit."

"Neither. I just did my job."

"Not according to the news report. They said you single-handedly overcame tremendous obstacles, including organized crime and the police, to get the full story."

"Don't believe everything you hear on the news."

"I don't, but apparently Rocky does. And if he has half as many creeps working for him out there as the news credits him with, I'd say your chances right now are worth about two cents, considering inflation."

He wouldn't get any argument from her on that score. She'd been thinking exactly that ever since she'd left the diner with her uninvited guest. But she'd focused her fears on her abductor, not on Rocky. And, for now, one threat on her life was all she could handle.

"I think we'd both better get a little rest while we can." His voice softened. "It'll be dark early with all this rain. As soon as it is, we'll get back on the road, put some more distance between us and New Orleans. It's not too safe for either of us right now."

"Wait a minute." Melissa wasn't going to let him off that easily. "What happened to our deal?"

"Deal?"

"Right. Now it's my turn to hear about you. It's kind of unfair, don't you think, for you to know all about me when I don't even know your name."

"I told you. I don't make deals. But my name's Brett, if that'll make you feel better. Now, why don't you lie down and try to get some sleep?"

"Brett what?"

"Look, lady, the less you know about me, the better off we'll both be. You can have the bed."

He collapsed into the chair and slipped his feet from a pair of Italian leather boots. "And remember, I'm a light sleeper," he mumbled, his eyes already closing. He stuffed his hands in his jacket pocket, the right one resting on the dreaded gun.

Melissa pulled back the spread and inspected the sheets. They were old and worn but evidently clean. She stretched out across the lumpy bed and rested her head on one of the pillows. Rest, sleep. Just the thought sounded divine, but she didn't dare close her eyes.

She didn't dare miss her chance to escape.

The door key might be safely stored in his jeans pocket, but the car keys were in plain sight on the table beside him. All she had to do was retrieve the keys, open the window and climb to safety.

She lay quietly and listened to the sound of the falling rain. The minutes ticked by, then stretched into hours. Still Brett wasn't asleep, at least not soundly. The rhythm of his breathing was too unsteady. But she'd outlast him. She had too much at stake not to.

A chill hung heavy in the room, and Melissa wrapped herself in the spread. She wouldn't sleep. She'd just close her eyes for a few seconds. They were so heavy, like a curtain closing on the final act.

The rain continued to fall, and she was back at home in her garden, sleeping in the giant swaying hammock between two creaking live oaks. And then there was nothing, nothing but silence and darkness...and sleep.

A car door slammed in the distance, and Melissa bolted upright. The room had grown dark, but the lumpy bed beneath her and the pungent odors of the unfamiliar surroundings jolted her to full wakefulness in a heartbeat. She listened for the easy breathing that would signal Brett's sleeping.

She listened, but the only sounds were the gentle creakings of the building itself. Slowly her eyes adjusted to the twilight darkness. The chair was empty. She swept her gaze around the room, searching for any sign of Brett. Nothing. There was nothing.

Thank God, there was nothing.

He'd probably slipped out as she slept. Probably taken her car with him, but she didn't care. Cars were replaceable. Her life wasn't.

She scooted from the bed and tiptoed toward the table where her keys had been. They were still there. Carefully she picked them up and placed them in her pocket, her heart nearly jumping from her throat as two keys rattled together noisily.

She took a deep breath, telling herself to relax. He was gone now.

Or was he merely outside the door?

Trembling, she found the phone and lifted the receiver. Dead. She guided her fingers along the cord until she reached the ends, cut and dangling in midair.

She crept to the window. Her car was barely visible in the faint glow of a blinking vacancy sign. But it was there, and she had the keys.

She unlocked the window and pushed upward. Stuck. She bit back the curse that flew to her lips.

Brett seemed to think of everything. Cut telephone wires, stuck windows, and without a doubt he'd locked the door and taken the key.

Well, that wouldn't be enough to slow her down for long. She had a healthy set of lungs, and when she finished yelling, there wouldn't be a person in the whole motel who didn't know where she was. And if that didn't work, she'd break the window and crawl through.

Still, it wouldn't hurt to try the easy way first. She twisted the doorknob and pulled. Startled, she jumped back as a blast of cold, wet air struck her in the face.

Well, what do you know? Even old Brett sometimes made mistakes. The thought pleased her immensely.

Pulling her coat about her tightly, she grabbed her purse and ran for her car. The driveway gravel shifted beneath her feet, but somehow she kept her balance, reaching the car in seconds.

"Melissa!" A man's voice cracked through the night air.

She fumbled, her shaking hands trying desperately to fit the key into the lock.

"Melissa! Don't open that door. Wait. Melissa!"

The voice was closer now, but the key was turning. She jerked the door open as two large hands pulled her from the car, pushing her away, throwing her down into the cold mud.

She tried to scream, but the fall had taken her breath. Pain coursed through her body. He was on top of her now, crushing her beneath him, his hands covering her mouth, her whole face.

And then the world exploded around her.

Chapter Three

An explosion like nothing Melissa had ever imagined filled the once quiet night with the sound and light of a thousand Independence Days.

Rain pelted the ground around her, but the rain was no longer only water. It was arrows of burning metal and jagged glass. And the rain was bloodred.

She screamed, and her cries mingled with curses, the curses of the man who held her captive in this fiery hell.

"Are you hurt?" Brett yelled above the fireworks.

Melissa stared in shock at the blood pooling around her. She didn't feel any pain, though. She didn't feel anything at all.

"I don't know. I don't think so," she answered shakily.

"Thank God." He rolled away. "We've got to get out of here. Now!" He grabbed her arm and pulled her to her feet.

Her legs wobbled beneath her, and she fell against him. "I can't." She fought back the tears. "If you're going to shoot me, do it now. I've had all I can take."

His arm wound around her protectively. He took her chin in his hand and turned her face toward a burning mass, toward what was, until a moment ago, her bright red sports car.

"Honey, if I wanted to do you in, I'd have to stand in line." He tore a piece of his shirttail and dabbed at a stream of blood trickling down her forehead.

"My car. That's my car." She whispered the words, the shock of what had happened seeping slowly into her consciousness. "Why would someone blow up my car?"

"I don't know, but I don't think this is a good time to hang around and ask questions." He tugged at her arm, forcing her to follow him toward the back corner of the parking lot.

Melissa allowed herself to be dragged along, but her gaze remained glued to the exploded mass, her brain trying desperately to make sense out of chaos. Someone blew up her car, all right. But not intentionally. They didn't care about her car at all. It was her they'd meant to blow to smithereens.

The shaking overtook her then. And the cold. The chill started deep inside and inundated her whole body with a frosty fear. And then she picked up speed, running as if from the devil himself, clasping Brett's hand, following her abductor without thinking.

In seconds they reached a dark blue car. Brett flung open the door on the passenger side and pushed her inside. He flew to the driver's side and slipped behind the wheel.

"Mighty thoughtful friend you have. He even left us the key."

The words fell on her ears without meaning, but then nothing seemed to make sense. A few minutes ago she was running away from Brett. Running in terror. Now she was running away with him.

He turned the car around and headed down the drive at breakneck speed, skimming the wet surface like a ship at sea. Melissa sank into her seat and closed her eyes. She didn't want to look ahead, didn't want to wonder where they were going, or why.

And she didn't want to look back.

But she did. It was as if she was moving in a dream. She had to turn back, had to see the glow from what used to be her car. The car she was meant to be in.

"Don't look. Just fasten that seat belt and try to pull yourself together. You're safe now."

His voice was strong and reassuring. Melissa took deep breaths, trying to slow her racing pulse. Safe? How could she be safe? Her life was spiraling out of control.

She stared at the man behind the wheel. His trembling had ceased completely, and the firm set of his jaw left no room for doubt about who was in control.

In control and in excruciating pain.

Blood was smeared across his face and matted in his sun-bleached hair. It trickled down his arm and down the front of his trousers where his torn shirttail hung loose. It soaked through the back of his nylon jacket, painting a growing circle of dark stain on the rough fabric of the car seat.

He tried to lean back, but each attempt brought more blood, more pain. He winced, but didn't cry out.

"You've got to see a doctor."

"No! No doctors."

Melissa started to argue, but one look and she knew it would be useless. His mouth was clamped shut, his eyes staring straight ahead. He was a strong man. It was written in every line of his face. Strong and stubborn. No amount of arguing would change his mind.

He pulled into the interstate traffic and fell in behind another car. He wasn't speeding, wasn't doing anything to alert a passing motorist or perhaps a policeman that something might be amiss.

They were just a couple on the road in the gathering darkness. Just a couple. Only one part of the couple had slivers of glass and who knew what else imbedded in his back. And the other was in limbo, vacillating between the blurred state of shock and the even more confusing state of reality.

Reality. She had to face it, had to get a grip on things. She stared at the man beside her, at the fighting tilt of his head, the determination that overpowered his pain.

Who was he really? And what did he want from her?

A few hours ago he'd appeared from nowhere. He'd stuck a gun in her ribs and made his will hers. With raw strength and a weapon of death, he'd forced her to obey his commands.

He'd saved her life.

An icy tingle crept up her spine. She'd been inches from death. Mere inches. She felt the beating of her heart deep within her chest.

The feeling was wonderful.

"Thanks." The word caught in the lump in her throat and came out as little more than a whisper.

"Thanks?" he questioned, incredulity coloring his tone.

"You saved my life."

"I owed you one."

"You could've been killed."

"But I wasn't," he answered, as matter-of-factly as if they were discussing the weather.

"Anyway, thanks."

"My pleasure." He turned toward her, but the touch of rough fabric on his shoulder caused him to catch his breath in pain. "Well, not exactly pleasure."

"Brett." She said his name tentatively. It felt strange on her tongue. He was the enemy, the kidnapper. She must not forget that, must not let any familiarity develop between them. It wouldn't be safe.

"Yes?"

"How did you know? I mean what made you think the car would blow like that?"

"Accident. Fate. Being in the right place at the right time. Maybe all of the above."

"I don't understand."

"I was cutting out. I'd gone out to the parking lot thinking I could hot-wire somebody's car, hit the road and drive into Houston. Once there, I'd ditch the car. I'd be through with it before the owner even missed it."

Melissa waited for more, her reporter's mind eagerly sweeping the cobwebs of shock away now that there were pieces to the puzzle.

"And?" she questioned, impatiently.

"And you'd be free to go on your way. I figured you had enough problems with Rocky. You didn't need me."

"No, I mean and what happened next? Did you actually see the guy who rigged the car?"

"I saw him, all right. I watched him get out of this car and slink around to your car. Once he'd put his little surprise in place he hightailed it into those bushes behind the parking lot. It didn't take a genius to figure out that a man sneaking around in the rain was up to no good."

No, not a genius, Melissa agreed silently. All it took was another man up to no good, but this was not the time to get into that.

"Did he see you?"

"No. I guess I'm a better sneak than he is."

"This is nothing to joke about. That man meant to kill me. And you didn't even wake me up to tell me. What if you hadn't stopped me in time? I mean you almost let me—"

"Hey, hold on a minute. What happened to the humble thanks I was getting a few minutes ago?"

"I don't know. I need answers, Brett." Her head ached now, ached from being thrown to the ground, from a day of tension, from an overwhelming sense of helplessness.

It was more than just the danger. In her profession, danger was part of the overhead, one of the costs of running the business. But it usually led to some way of finding the facts.

With Brett, she'd been banging her head against a brick wall from the very first. No wonder it ached.

"Where are we going now?" she questioned.

"I wish to hell I knew."

And so did Melissa. He was running from something—or someone. That was certain, but nothing else was. She was lost in a fog of confusion, and she'd had enough. It was definitely time to talk.

"Brett, a few minutes ago you risked your life to save mine. Now it's time to take another risk. You've got to trust someone to help you get out of this trouble you're in." Without thinking, Melissa placed her hand on his arm as she spoke. His muscles tensed, as if ready for a fight.

She withdrew her hand and plunged ahead with her offer. "That someone might as well be me."

"It's not a pretty story, Melissa. Are you sure you want to hear it?"

Melissa. Funny, she'd wanted him to call her by name earlier, wanted him to think of her as a real person and not just someone to be used and destroyed. Now she wasn't sure.

Her kidnapper had risked his life for hers. He was talking to her, calling her by name, like an old friend. But there was something more to this new familiarity that seemed to be forging between them. It was the absence of fear, healthy fear that would keep her on her toes. Keep her alive.

She shook her head to clear away the mass of bewildering thoughts.

"I don't blame you, and I'm not going to force my problems on you," he continued in a husky voice, mistaking her head shake for an answer.

"I want to hear them," she assured him. "I can handle problems. It's not knowing what's going on that's making me a basket case. Besides, I deserve to know what we're faced with. Like it or not, I'm right in the middle of it."

"Okay. Here goes." He took a deep breath. "I'm a fugitive...from a mental hospital."

He paused, and Melissa knew he was waiting for a gasp, a cry, some outward sign of her feelings. She faced him squarely. "Go on."

"Go on?"

"Right. Get on with the story. Why were you there and how and when did you get out?"

"I was there because my dearly beloved sister-in-law was afraid I was getting too close to the truth about my brother's death."

His tone grew cold and hard. Melissa waited silently. He was obviously dealing with feelings that were far more painful than the cuts and scratches on his bleeding skin.

"I honestly don't remember how I got to the hospital, but I'm sure it was her doing. I'd been in the garden all day, trying to piece together what happened the last days before Jason's death. He'd wanted me there. I should have known that from his first letter. He needed someone there he could trust."

"I don't understand. Was your brother ill?"

"He'd been sick for several weeks. He said it was the flu, some rare strain. I don't remember, Asian, African, whatever. When he first contacted me about it, I just figured he'd be fine in a day or two. I never gave it much thought."

Brett hammered his fist against the steering wheel. "If I'd taken time to call him, I might have realized something was going on between him and that golddigger wife of his. And he might be alive today."

His voice caught in a sob. He turned it into a curse.

Melissa fought the urge to reach out to him. She didn't want to feel his grief. She needed to stay separated from this man. She wanted the facts, nothing more.

"She killed him," he continued, control returning to his voice. "I don't know how yet, but I know she did it. And she knows I won't rest as long as she goes free."

"Was his death ruled a homicide?"

"Oh, no. Dear wifey covered her tracks far too well to fall under suspicion. Heart failure, that's what the death was ruled."

"Then how can you be so sure it was murder?"

"It's all here. In Jason's letters." Brett reached under his shirt and pulled out a blood-stained plastic bag stuffed with folded envelopes. "The answers are somewhere in these letters. And in the diary."

"You mean you have your brother's diary?"

"No. But I know where it is. At least I know it's hidden somewhere in the garden. Near the roses, I think. The letter said..."

Brett rubbed his forehead as if trying to remember. "It's the drugs. Those damn drugs. A thought, a word can be right there and then you lose it."

Melissa felt his anguish. She didn't know if his story was true, but she was sure it was true in his mind. He was tortured by his brother's death.

But he'd be even more tortured if he didn't get help soon. He needed different drugs now. Something for the pain and something for the infection that was sure to come.

"Brett, you need help. I know it's difficult for you to think clearly right now, but you have to listen to me. Your injuries are going to get a whole lot worse unless you get them cleaned up and treated. You need medicine, an antibiotic. You need it now."

"Don't worry about me. I'll be fine." His shoulder brushed the seat as he spoke and he tried unsuccessfully to hide the pain. "A few aspirin and a couple of days' rest. I'll be good as new. It's you we have to worry about."

"Me? What do you mean?"

"Don't tell me you've forgotten already. Some sleaze ball out there wants you dead. His car bomb didn't work, but those crazies don't give up. He'll try again. Too bad I didn't get my hands on him this time."

Suddenly Melissa was aware of the cold, the bitter cold of her skin beneath the wet clothes. She didn't want to think of bombs and crazies. She didn't want to deal with kidnappers and mental patients.

"We have to call the police, Brett."

"I don't think that's a good idea."

"It's the only way. I'll talk to them, tell them you saved my life. They'll check your story out, and they'll help." Her voice broke, but she had to go on, had to convince him it was the only answer. For both of them.

"Melissa, Rocky was the leader of the New Orleans police force. He must have connections everywhere."

"Not everywhere. I know some officers. They'll help you. They'll help us. I promise."

"No. I've had my fill of the criminal justice system already. Their brand of justice locked me away while my brother's murderer paraded the streets of Baton Rouge like a benevolent queen."

"They made a mistake, but—"

"Melissa, I know you're still reeling from everything that's happened, but you have to be very careful. The man at the motel was no ordinary crazy. I didn't want to tell you this. I was afraid it would frighten you even more."

"Tell me what?" she insisted.

"He was a cop. At least he was dressed in a dark blue uniform with some kind of insignia on the sleeve."

"I don't believe you. You would have said so earlier. You're just afraid of what will happen to you if I call the police, and you're trying to scare me."

"You're right. I'm trying to scare some sense into you. And if you don't plan to be one of Rocky's last victims, you'd better listen."

"I'm listening." But she didn't want to. She longed to close her ears and mind to his words.

She wanted to, but she didn't dare. Rocky had gained his control over the drug business by being tougher and more violent than the dealers. He'd taken his cut from every major deal that came down, and he'd done it with the paid help of his "special forces."

"I don't know why I picked you up today, Melissa, except that I was desperate. I had to get out of town fast, before I was missed and somebody put out a bulletin to have me tracked down and brought back to that so-called hospital."

Melissa could tell he was groping for the right words. She waited quietly, giving him a chance to say his piece.

"Anyway, to make a long story short, I'm sorry for all that I put you through. On the other hand, if I hadn't been with you, you'd be..."

"I'd be dead."

"Right. Whoever wanted you dead had to be following your car. And now he'll be looking for this one."

"Maybe he thinks I'm dead, that I blew up in the explosion."

"Not a chance. That bomb wasn't rigged to the engine. If it had been, it wouldn't have gone off until you switched on the ignition. It had to be a simple remote-control device. He orchestrated the whole thing, from beginning to end."

"And you think he'll be coming after me again?"

"No reason to think he wouldn't. But I doubt if he'll do it right away. He's probably heading back to town about now, trying to set up an alibi that places him far away from the bombing. That's one thing in your favor. The other is that he won't be reporting his car as missing. Not from the...the Stop 'N Sleep Motel where Melissa Bentley's car just...just took to the sky."

His words began to slur, and his hands shook on the wheel. The car swerved into the next lane before he could pull it back again. Still, what he said made sense. Too much sense. He had everything wrapped up in a neat little package. He even had himself sounding like the hero. But he'd omitted one little step.

"So, why don't you just drop me off in the next town? I have friends I can call. They'll pick me up. I'll be on my way, and you can be on yours."

"That's fine, Melissa. Whatever you want." His voice faltered and broke.

The light from a passing car illuminated his face. He had grown ghostly pale. Beads of sweat dotted his brow, and his right hand clutched his head as if providing its only support.

"Pull over, Brett."

"You can't get out here. We're in the middle of nowhere."

"I'm not getting out. I'm changing places with you. You're hurt. You've lost a lot of blood. You can't keep driving."

Melissa breathed a sigh of relief as he slipped his foot onto the brake and slowed the car to a crawl, easing onto the shoulder of the highway. He was fighting to stay alert, but he was fighting a losing battle. He braked with a jolt, and his body slumped against the steering wheel.

Melissa unclasped the seat belt and opened her door. A cold wind whipped at her short curls and cut through her damp clothing like daggers of ice. It awakened her senses, setting her mind in motion.

She glanced at Brett. He'd given in to the fatigue, the nausea, or was it to pure pain? It didn't matter. His head rested against the steering wheel, his eyes closed.

Pulses racing, Melissa reached toward him. She held her breath and whispered a silent prayer as she eased her hand into his jacket pocket. The metal was cold, forbidding, but she wrapped her fingers around the pistol.

He twitched in pain, and her heart slammed against her ribs. But he only moaned softly, his body lost in its own torment.

The gun was hers.

She closed the door behind her and gulped in the fresh air, filling her lungs with its crispness. A feeling of control grew and seemed to encompass her, making her strong and solid, like the pavement beneath her feet.

She'd followed someone else's bidding for hours, followed it because she'd had no choice. But that was over. Brett had held her life in his hands, and he'd risked his life to save hers. She was grateful. Grateful, but not stupid. And not helpless.

She'd be making the decisions now.

Chapter Four

Melissa walked quickly to the driver's side of the compact car, the gun heavy in her trembling hand. She reached out for Brett and nudged him gently. He groaned weakly, but dragged his body across the bloodstained seat.

She slipped out of her raincoat and draped it across the seat, thankful for the heavy vinyl that acted as a shield between her and the fresh blood. She slid behind the wheel, praying that he'd pass out without noticing the missing gun.

He leaned back against the seat, then closed his eyes. Cautiously, she moved the gun to her left hand and placed it on the seat beside her. A shudder escaped her lips. Even against the thick fabric of her sweats, it felt cold and evil.

She took a deep breath. She had the gun, but if her luck held she wouldn't have to use it. Brett was quiet, in severe pain and apparently lost in his own secret nightmares.

Melissa flipped on the radio searching for some soft music to soothe her nerves. She expected too much. The voice blaring from the speaker was not melodic and definitely not soothing.

"Rocky Matherne, the incumbent sheriff of New Orleans, had been expected to win tomorrow's election by a landslide. Instead, he is behind bars tonight, although he continues to deny all accusations against him."

She switched the radio off.

Rocky could deny all he wanted, if it made him happy, but that wouldn't change the facts. There was enough evidence against him to lock him up and throw away the key. She had worked on the case night and day for the past four months, barely taking time to eat and sleep. But knowing he was behind bars made all her efforts worthwhile.

The facts she'd uncovered about his reign of power were grisly. Blackmail, murder, torture. Nothing had been beyond him. He took what he wanted, and heaven help any innocent citizen who stood in his way.

"In jail, but still doing his dirty work. You took on one tough son of a...one tough guy, lady." Brett's words were slow, edged with the pain that ran roughshod through his body. "You got some kind of death wish?"

"I told you. I was just doing my job. I'm not a hero."

"No, I didn't say you were a hero. Just another half-baked reporter out to dig up the dirt."

Melissa grimaced. Brett was not as out of it as she'd hoped. Too bad. She could do without his comments. They rankled her already raw nerves.

Besides, who was he to criticize? "And what about you?" she quipped. "Your life doesn't appear to be a bed of roses just now."

"You don't need to worry about me. I can take care of myself. I always have. Just drop me off anywhere."

His words slurred, and his head fell forward. "I just need some rest."

"You *need* a doctor."

"No." Renewed strength and determination seemed to surge through his body, and he lifted his head, turning to face her. "No doctors."

"Don't be ridiculous, Brett. Your injuries are not the sort that aspirin can cure."

"And that hellhole hospital I escaped from is no place to heal. I'm not going back." He cupped his large hand around her slender wrist. Even in his weakened condition, his strength wrapped around her threateningly. "I'm *not* going back."

Melissa felt for the gun, stroking the cold metal. She cursed herself silently. Why should she care what happened to this man? She could do just as she wished. Her common sense told her to drop him off somewhere and let him fend for himself.

She tapped her fingers against the steering wheel. But she wouldn't. The man was wounded and he needed help. More to the point, he'd been injured while saving her life.

No. She had no choice. Fate had linked them together, and for now he was her responsibility. She had to find some way to get him the care he needed.

She was in control, she reminded herself. She could use the pistol, if she had to, but only to save her life. Not to force her will on someone else. She couldn't make him seek medical help.

There had to be some other way. She lowered the window a crack. She needed fresh air, needed to think clearly. Brett's fears were not unfounded, and she knew it. If she took him to an emergency room, there would

be questions. Lots of them. And there would be a police report, and a one-way trip to the mental hospital.

She wasn't sure he was telling the truth, but then, she
wasn't sure he was lying, either. The gun gave her a
measure of control, but her conscience didn't leave her
a lot of choices. She'd just have to think of something.
Someplace they could go where she'd be out of danger
from the crackpot who wanted her dead. Someplace
where Brett could get the medical help he needed without detection.

She shook her head doubtfully, going over all the
places in her mind that wouldn't work. "So where do
we go from here, Brett? You seem to have all the answers."

But once again the mystery man beside her was silent. He remained slumped in the seat, his eyes closed,
his body still except for an occasional tightening of
muscles as he fought the pain. Right or wrong, the decisions would all be hers.

She continued west, the lines of Interstate 10 falling
away behind her, the motion and darkness lulling her
into a dangerous sense of security. There was nowhere
to go, nothing to do but drive on and on with only the
occasional lights from an oncoming vehicle to break the
monotony.

Gradually the rain slowed to a gentle mist, and the
tightness in her muscles gave way once more to pure
weariness. She was drifting, floating somewhere between rational wakefulness and the beginnings of sleep.
She lowered the window a few inches more. She needed
the sting of cold air on her face and in her lungs.

But even that wasn't enough to shake her to full
alertness. Her thoughts drifted to a quieter time, a time

when she'd played along the edge of Bayou Lachere, happily watching the mist roll off the still waters.

Her grandmother's bayou cabin had always been a haven for Melissa, a place where time seemed to stand still, where days blended into nights with only the song of the crickets and the dancing of fireflies to herald their passing. A place so isolated from the bustle of civilization that one almost forgot there were people in the world besides her grandmother.

Her grandmother and Cotile. One never forgot persnickety old Aunt Cotile.

Suddenly, Melissa's mind shifted into high gear. The cabin. That was the answer she'd been searching for. A place even Rocky's thugs wouldn't be able to find. A place where Brett could have time to heal.

She pulled the car into the right lane, and her stomach drew into an unexpected knot. She hadn't been to the cabin since the aftermath of the Robert Galliano affair. She'd come a long way toward putting the hurt behind her, but going there now was bound to open old wounds.

She gripped the wheel tightly and swerved into the exit lane. She'd made it through the last few hours. She'd certainly make it through a few old memories.

Of course going to the cabin also meant they'd have to reverse their direction, head into Louisiana and the area they'd fled from only a couple of hours ago. Still, with any luck they'd reach the safety of the cabin before sunup.

She'd take the back roads. There were miles of them, dark and nearly isolated, passing through small Cajun villages and edging along boggy marshes. She'd just head southeast until she reached familiar territory.

Brett shifted and moaned softly at the car's movements, and Melissa placed her right hand on his. "Everything's all right," she murmured, but the tremble in her voice betrayed her words. She whispered the words again, this time determined to believe them herself.

HOURS LATER Melissa turned onto the narrow dirt road that skirted the cypress-dotted swampland and wound toward the banks of Bayou Lachere. The skies had cleared, and the moon dipped through the branches of the towering trees. She was thankful for that. Otherwise even her knowledgeable eyes would have had difficulty sighting the familiar landmark.

But there it was, the twisted old tree. Disfigured by lightning, growing almost parallel to the ground, it signaled the way to the cabin. She turned in, praying the old logging road had not been washed away by the fall rains.

Her brother had filled in the road more times than she could count, persistently insuring that the path to his precious hunting grounds was preserved.

She'd always hated the thought of him and his friends visiting her childhood haven with their guns, killing the animals that had more right to the place than any human ever had. But for once, she was thankful for his diligent efforts. The cabin was ahead of her, framed in the moonlight, and the road was firm beneath the tires.

Melissa slowed the car to a crawl and stopped at the end of the road. Somehow she'd have to get Brett the next twenty yards or so on foot. She switched off the engine and the headlights.

An owl hooted in the distance, an eerie reminder of the seclusion she'd invaded. The hairs on Melissa's neck stood on end. She'd made it to her destination safely, but there were no feelings of relief to sweeten her arrival. Instead, the emotions that permeated her senses were strange and chilling.

She was alone. Alone on the very edge of civilization. Brett stirred beside her.

No. Not alone. That was the problem. Alone she would have felt safe, embraced by the darkness, comforted by the familiar sounds of the bayou at night.

Melissa opened the door and forced her legs to move, to climb from the car and tackle whatever lay ahead. She'd made her decision, and this was not the time for regrets. It was the time for action—cool, clearheaded action.

Slipping the gun into the pocket of her raincoat, she pulled the heavy vinyl wrap across her shoulders. Her feet sank in the moist earth, but she made her way through the overgrowth and over to Brett's door.

She shook him gently. "This is it, Brett. You'll have to help me get you inside."

He opened his eyes and looked around. His body began to shake, and he grabbed her arm, pulling her to him. "We can't stay here, Melissa. Get back in the car."

His eyes were glazed, his body obviously tortured by pain and the serious loss of blood, his mind still suffering from too many drugs for far too long.

But he was conscious. Thank heavens for that. She'd never have been able to drag a man his size up the steps and into the cabin.

"We'll be safe here, Brett. Just slide over and lean on me." She kept her voice low and as calming as she could manage. "We'll get you inside...and into bed."

"Who lives here?" His voice was heavy, his words dragging like a record played at slow speed.

"No one. The cabin's empty. It has been for the last eight years. You'll be safe. We both will."

Melissa breathed a small sigh of relief as Brett let go of her arm and gingerly scooted his feet around and tried to stand. He held on to the door, his hand shaking, his body limp. Melissa moved quickly to his side, placing her arm around him for support.

He pulled away. "I'm okay. I can make it on my own. Just give me a minute."

He took a step, and Melissa watched the moonlight play across the ghostlike pallor of his face. He was fiercely independent. Whatever else he might be, she'd have to give him that.

Whatever else. An escapee from a mental hospital. A man who'd put a gun in her ribs and taken her hostage. She slipped her hand into her pocket, sliding her fingers across the gun's safety lever, reassuring herself of her control. Then she turned and walked slowly down the muddy path, giving Brett time to follow on his own.

He tripped over a rambling root and almost fell. Melissa turned to help him.

"I'll make it," he mumbled. He stumbled off the path to lean on a wooden picnic table that nestled beneath a towering cypress tree.

"Okay, take your time. I'll go ahead and get the lights."

The key turned easily. Melissa hesitated, listening for any sound that might suggest someone had arrived before them.

But all was quiet.

She was getting paranoid. Not that there wasn't plenty of reason to be after the events of the last twenty-four hours. Still, it wasn't like her. She pushed open the door and stepped inside.

Dank, musty odors rose to choke her. She coughed and then stiffened. Something moved near her foot. Or was it only a shadow?

One hand on the trigger, she slid the other hand over the bare wooden walls until her fingers brushed across the plastic switch. Instantly, it responded to her touch, flooding the room with light.

"They grow 'em big around here, don't they?" Brett pushed through the door just in time to see their welcoming party.

"Too big," Melissa whispered, her color returning as two giant Louisiana cockroaches scurried beneath the couch. Murderers and escaped psychos she might be able to handle. But cockroaches? Never.

Brett stumbled toward the couch. "They can join me if they like, just so they leave enough room for me. All I want is rest."

"Not yet. Those wounds need to be dressed. There's bound to be some first-aid stuff around here somewhere, if I can just find where those guys stashed it."

"Guys?" Alarm temporarily sharpened his drugged senses. "I thought you said no one ever comes here."

"I said no one *lives* here. My brother and his pals come down here regularly to fish. Or to hunt."

"Hunters. Just what I need."

He reached into his jacket pocket, the one where he kept his gun. His expression changed in an instant, the rugged lines in his face growing hard as steel.

Melissa's heart pounded painfully against her chest, but she stood her ground, her finger against the trigger, poised for action. She had to maintain control. It was her only salvation.

"I have the gun, Brett."

"Give it back." He reached toward her, but he lost his balance, falling against the back of the couch. "Damn it, Melissa. Keep the gun." He hurled the words at her in a fit of frustration. "It doesn't really matter who has it, anyway."

Doesn't matter? His words made no sense at all. It mattered, all right. And she was not about to hand the gun over. Even if Brett was a decent man under ordinary circumstances, that wouldn't mean a thing now.

"I'll get out tomorrow, Melissa. You'll have to leave, too. It isn't safe here. But it should be okay for tonight. Just to..." His words drifted off into nothingness, his knees gave way, and he sank onto the couch.

"Here, Brett, let me help you. The bed will be a lot more comfortable than that lumpy sofa."

This time he didn't fight it. He placed his arm around her shoulder, and she guided him to the next room. With one hand, she yanked back the chenille spread and the top sheet as Brett collapsed onto the bed.

Eyes closed, he hardly seemed to notice as she tugged the expensive leather boots from his feet and the light Windbreaker from his bruised shoulders. The bleeding had almost stopped, and his breathing seemed less labored. He'd rest. Probably for a long time.

Melissa felt the tenseness ebb from her aching muscles as she pulled the door shut behind her. For the first time in hours, she moved without fear. She longed to grab a shower and snuggle under a ton of quilts in her grandmother's four-poster bed.

But she couldn't. Not yet. Not until she'd found those aspirins Brett thought would provide a magical cure. And something to cleanse his wounds. She walked to the kitchen, turning on the light before she entered, giving any crawling guests enough time to hide. Life on the bayou did have some disadvantages.

She took off her raincoat and slung it across a straight-backed chair. The kitchen was strangely comforting. Virtually unchanged in the eight years since her grandmother's death, it was as simple and functional as ever. Just the way Gramme had liked it.

The same beat-up coffeepot rested on the range top, and the petite wooden oar Melissa's grandfather had once carved for his bride's new pirogue stood in the corner by the back door.

She opened the cabinet above the sink. Colorful mugs and flowered plates stared at her from their neat rows. But patterned dishes were not what she needed.

She moved around the room, opening one cabinet after another, searching for anything to assuage Brett's pain. There was a bottle of aspirin and a fifth of whiskey in one cabinet. She took them both.

She searched further, climbing on one of the chairs to reach the highest cabinets. Even though they were out of reach for her, they were well within the reach of her six-foot-three-inch brother. Just the place he might store seldom-used first-aid supplies.

But the shelves were empty, except for a couple of cans of red spray paint and an old claw hammer.

An agonized moan drifted from the bedroom. Quickening her pace, Melissa hurried down the dark hall to the one small bathroom. The closet in there was enormous, and it had always been the catch-all corner. If you didn't know where else to stash something, throw it in the bathroom.

She opened the closet door and was met with the usual mass of clutter. The one closet even her grandmother had given up on, overpowered by the rest of the family's need to hoard half-empty containers and worn-out equipment.

And supplies. Best of all supplies, she acknowledged, as she spied a cardboard box on the floor, the words "first aid" scribbled on the side with a black marking pen. Thankfully, she pulled it out.

It held one container after another. They all bore the same familiar warning. "In case of serious injury, see your physician immediately."

Oh, well, it wouldn't be the first warning she'd ignored.

An unopened package of latex gloves was stuffed behind an economy-size bottle of cherry-flavored cough syrup. She dropped the gloves into her pocket and rummaged until she found a small pair of scissors, a half-empty tube of antibiotic cream, an unopened bottle of peroxide and some adhesive tape. There was even a pair of tweezers. Probably the donation of some unlucky guest who'd scooted across the wooden porch swing.

She tucked her finds into an empty paper bag from one of the shelves and began going through the stacks of linens on the top two shelves. Her luck held. There was a supply of clean, white sheets, old and well worn, just the thing for tearing into strips. She draped one over her arm and added a couple of washcloths and a large terry towel. Now all she needed was a pan of warm water.

She started into the bedroom. The floor creaked beneath her, and she jumped instinctively, her heart leaping to her throat. She'd have to relax. They might be here for days, and she couldn't keep panicking at every new sound.

It was unlikely anyone could find her here. And Brett was harmless, wounded and barely conscious. Besides, the man couldn't be the monster he'd seemed at first. Monsters didn't risk their lives to save others. And, if he was telling the truth, he should never have been committed to the psychiatric hospital in the first place.

If he was telling the truth.

She spun, heading to the kitchen to retrieve the gun before beginning her nursing chores. It might be safe enough here, but caution was always wise.

Safe? Was that really why she'd come here tonight, or did something stronger always draw her to the bayou in time of trouble?

She'd come here three years ago when her world had fallen apart, when she'd learned that every word out of Robert Galliano's mouth had been nothing more than cruel lies. Learned that every touch, every kiss, every whisper of love had been meted out with measured accuracy, the poignant poison of a mind ruled by the quest for power.

And she'd believed his lies. Believed them until they'd almost destroyed her completely. Now she was at the cabin with another man. A man with stories of his own. And she had no way of knowing if those stories were true or only figments of a drug-enhanced imagination.

She wanted to believe him. She wasn't sure why.

Maybe it was because he'd saved her life. Or perhaps it was the raw emotion that choked his voice when he talked about his brother. Or the intensity with which he fought returning to the hospital.

Or maybe it was just her own gullibility. The same gullibility that had let her fall victim to the wrong man once before.

But it could have happened just as Brett described it, she assured herself. In this world anything could happen. And often did. If nothing else, her years as an investigative reporter had taught her that.

Good or bad, there was a story here. And, given time, she'd get to the bottom of it. For now, all she had to do was stay alert. And alive.

She collected the gun and water and then, arms and pockets laden with supplies, she tiptoed into the bedroom and flicked on the lamp. Golden streams of light spread across the bed, and Brett groaned in protest, moving a bruised hand to cover his eyes.

He was lying on his stomach, his huge frame almost covering the bed. His shirt was ripped, revealing the injuries inflicted by fragments of flying glass and metal.

Melissa tensed. He'd shielded her from this, willingly taking the brunt of the explosion. An explosion that had been meant for her. Only whoever had planted the bomb had not planned on leaving survivors. He had wanted her dead. And there was no reason to believe that one setback had altered his desire.

She shook her head, determined to put those thoughts out of her mind. Brett had saved her life. She owed him the best care she could provide. No matter how much he protested.

Melissa helped him roll over enough to lift his head. She placed the aspirin in his parched mouth and held a glass of cool water to his lips. He sipped slowly, some of the water trickling down the stubble of dark hair that peppered his chin. She brushed the drops away and then urged him to take a few swallows of the whiskey. It was the closest thing to a painkiller she'd been able to find.

He drained the last drops of whiskey from the glass and sank back onto the soft mattress, mumbling something that sounded like thanks.

As gently as possible, Melissa removed the shirt from his body, cutting it when necessary to avoid unnecessary pain. She dipped the clean cloth into a pan of warm water and touched it to his flesh. He groaned softly but didn't roll away.

"This is going to hurt, I know, Brett, but I have to do it. I'll be as gentle as possible. Just try to relax."

She moved the damp cloth across his broad shoulders. He jerked and tightened his muscles, his reaction guiding her to the small piece of jagged glass imbedded in his flesh. Melissa took the tweezers and pulled it out, gritting her teeth as Brett flinched in pain.

She continued, bathing each area slowly, scrutinizing each sound Brett made, each movement, until she'd removed more than half a dozen foreign objects from his skin. The largest had been a piece of twisted metal, buried in the flesh of his right shoulder.

He'd been the perfect patient, sucking up the pain like a man of steel. He'd even felt like a man of steel. His body was firm, his muscles strong and unyielding. But even a man of steel had to have his limits.

"I'm almost through now, Brett," she soothed. "Just a few minutes more. You'll feel something running down your back. Don't worry. It's just peroxide. It'll wash out the open wounds and kill the germs."

"Not germs," he protested suddenly, his tone insistent. "She didn't kill the germs. She killed Jason. Why can't you people understand? She killed Jason."

Melissa didn't know about Brett's sister-in-law, but she was sure of one thing. This bottle of peroxide wasn't going to kill all the germs breeding in his gaping wounds. He'd have to have some antibiotics, and soon. And a tetanus shot.

If he didn't get them, he wouldn't have to worry about Jason. He'd be joining him.

Melissa yawned. She was so tired. She'd apply the antibiotic cream and some bandages. Then she'd get some rest. Only a little. Just until the sun came up. Then, somehow, she'd have to find a doctor for Brett.

She taped the last bandage and then peeled the rubber gloves from her hands as she collapsed into the over-stuffed chair at his bedside. She really should get up and shower. Or at least climb into a bed.

Her body refused to move. She glanced at the clock on the wall. Ten to five. Almost daybreak. No wonder she was tired. She'd close her eyes for just a minute.

She didn't hear the clock strike five. And she didn't hear the footsteps in the hall.

Chapter Five

Melissa stared into Robert Galliano's steely gray eyes. They were mesmerizing, imploring her to follow him. He took her hand, and his very touch set her on fire. She ran with him along the Gulf beach, her hair blowing freely, the pounding of the surf echoing the beating of her heart.

He stopped and took her in his arms, his hard body pressing against hers, his fingers caressing her, filling her with overpowering desire. Her body ached, consumed with the feel of him, the smell of him, the taste of him.

"You're mine, Melissa. Mine in every way." His arms tightened around her possessively.

"I love you, Robert."

"More than just love, Melissa. You *need* me. And I need you." His fingers traced the lines of her mouth before roving to her neck, stroking, gently at first, then growing harsh. "You belong to me, and you must never let me down."

"Please, don't talk this way. I love you, but you don't own me." She tried to pull away, but he wrapped her in his arms again, clutching her to him.

"You don't understand, do you, sweet Melissa? Your life is mine now. You must not fight it. It wouldn't be wise." He lowered his mouth to hers, brutally claiming her lips.

"Don't, Robert. Please. You're hurting me."

He laughed, a mirthless, ridiculing threat, and tightened his grasp.

She loved him so much, but he was leaving her no choice. She eased her hand into the pocket of her shorts and ran her fingers along the cold cylinder. The gun was still there, and she'd have to use it. There was no other way.

She pressed it to his ribs. "Look at me, Robert. See what you've turned me into."

But it wasn't Robert staring at her. It was Brett. His face was bleeding, and he was reaching out for her. "No... Sylvia."

Melissa bolted upright. Bright sunlight flooded the room, but there was no beach. She blinked repeatedly, trying desperately to clear her eyes and her mind. Where was she and why was her finger wrapped around the trigger of a gun?

A tormented voice cut through the thick haze of sleep. "Not Jason! Kill you...kill...Sylvia."

Terror gripped her heart, squeezing it like an overripe plum. Her finger tightened on the trigger, and she struggled to bring the room into focus.

"Murderer...no, no!"

Brett cried out again, but he still lay on the bed. His eyes were closed tightly, his body tense and strained, and his hands were curled into fists.

He was lost in a nightmare all his own, one she hoped she'd never have to share.

Melissa threw aside the quilt that covered her from neck to toe and stretched her cramped body. Funny, she remembered sinking into the overstuffed chair, remembered thinking she should get up and go to the other bedroom, but she didn't remember getting a quilt. It didn't make sense. If she'd gotten up to find a quilt, why wouldn't she have just gone down the hall and crawled into a comfortable bed?

Brett stirred and called out again. Melissa set the gun on the table and moved toward him. She touched his forehead. He was cool. No fever, at least not yet. But he'd lost a lot of blood last night. He'd be weak today and still in pain.

A pitcher of water sat on the table by his bed. She didn't remember putting that there, either, but she must have gotten it sometime during the night.

She glanced at her watch. Nine-thirty. She'd slept for hours. Still, Brett's cries must have wakened her enough to at least get him some water. So strange that she couldn't remember anything. Nothing. Nothing except smatterings of her distorted dream.

Brett jumped in his sleep as if startled and then flinched in pain as his bandaged shoulder rubbed the sheet. She placed her hand on his. "Brett, it's me, Melissa." She kept her voice low. She had to wake him, to release him from the dream's hold, but she didn't want to frighten him. And she definitely didn't want to be mistaken for this Sylvia person.

"It's all right. You're here at the cabin with me."

He opened his eyes, blinking them repeatedly. "Melissa?"

"Yes." She moved closer. "You got some nasty wounds last night. I removed several slivers of glass from your back and shoulders, but I may have missed

some. We can get a doctor if you need one." She made
the offer, although she had no doubt about his answer.

"No, the lady that was here..." He shook his head
and tried to raise his shoulders from the bed.

"Just try to relax, Brett. You can tell me about everything later." He was evidently still out of his head.
Probably thought he was in the hospital. She'd have to
be careful not to rile him. "Can I get you anything?"

"Water. Just water. I'm so thirsty."

Melissa filled the glass and placed it carefully in his
shaking hands. He turned the glass up, barely stopping
for breath as he gulped down the cool liquid.

Melissa shook three aspirin into her hand and slipped
them between his lips. "Here, these might help you feel
better."

He spit them into his hand. "What the hell are
these?"

"Just aspirin. If you don't want them, don't take
them. I'm not trying to force them on you."

Rolling them over in his hand, he examined the
markings carefully and then popped them in his mouth.
"Sorry. Guess I'm not too trusting these days."

No, and she wasn't, either. And it seemed they both
had darn good reasons. It was just too bad they were
stranded out here together. Of course, she wasn't the
one who'd initiated this bizarre relationship.

"Melissa." He whispered her name tentatively.

"Yes."

He rose up in the bed and stared at her. Hairs of bur-
nished gold danced across his broad chest, and once
again, Melissa was awed by the sheer maleness of him.

"Are you sure you're all right?"

"I'm fine. Thanks to you. You saved my life. If I'd gotten into that car, I'd be dead now." She shuddered. "Dead and scattered over the entire parish."

"Yeah. I thought maybe I'd bought the farm for a while there myself. The blood. It was everywhere."

"There was a scalp wound. Not serious, though it bled like crazy. Something grazed your head, a piece of metal from the looks of it, but it didn't penetrate. You have some other cuts and scratches on your back, though. They didn't bleed as much, but they may give you some trouble. You could use a tetanus shot. And an antibiotic."

Melissa tried to keep her voice calm, and she was amazed at her success. To a stranger, they might have been merely two close friends sharing their tales of horror. They might have been. But they weren't. The gun in her pocket was a constant reminder of that.

"What time is it?" Brett asked, throwing his feet across the side of the bed. "I've got to get moving. I should've been out of here hours ago." He tried to stand, but his knees and equilibrium didn't cooperate. He sat down on the soft mattress, the loss of blood still taking its toll.

"You're in no shape to go anywhere." Melissa cursed herself silently for her words. He wanted to leave. She should be helping him out the door.

"No. I have to go. She'll send them. Sylvia... lying murderer."

The shaking began again, and Melissa could make out only a few of Brett's words. Not that it mattered. His garbled accusations were no more meaningful than her dream had been. Just the crazed ramblings of an overwrought mind.

A mind coming off drugs. That was it. She'd never seen an addict coming down before, but she'd heard about them. The shaking, the thirst, the hallucinations. They were all here.

Even so, there was something about the man that fascinated her. Something strangely caring encased in a wild spirit. Over six feet tall, muscular and weathered, a modern-day Tarzan living in a jungle of murder and drugs. But a world not of his choosing, at least not if his story could be believed.

Holding his hand to his head, he fell back across the bed.

Melissa dampened a cloth and wiped it over his brow. "Try to rest now. I'll be here."

A trace of a smile crossed his lips as his lids drooped shut. Melissa sat by the bed and watched until his chest rose and fell rhythmically. A sigh of relief escaped her lips. She needed him to sleep, needed time to plot their next move.

Tiptoeing quietly, she made her way down the hall. She stopped in the back bedroom, the one she'd slept in as a child during countless long, lazy summers at Gramme's. She rummaged through the closet, through the rack of hanging clothes until she found a pair of faded jeans that looked to be about her size. Probably belonged to some kid who had come along with his father on one of her brother's hunting weekends.

She held the jeans up to her. The tiny waistline was accented with buttons, and a front yoke dropped below the hips. Scratch the kid idea. These were definitely the property of a stylish young woman. No wonder her brother spent so many weekends at the cabin.

Panic struck briefly. If Cody showed up now, she'd never be able to explain how she came to be at the cabin with an escapee from a mental hospital. But it was only Wednesday, she reassured herself. Even if he planned to come hunting this weekend he wouldn't arrive before Friday night. By then Brett would be miles away, and she'd be at home finding out what the devil was going on.

She'd find out who the rat was who'd set her up, and who he'd enlisted to do his murderous bidding. She'd even accept the assistance of the police if she had to, though she had a lot more faith in her own abilities. Funny, yesterday she'd needed a vacation. Today all she needed was facts.

No. That wasn't quite all. She needed a shower, a gloriously hot shower with tons of frothing soap and shampoo. She grabbed an oversize sweatshirt from the stack on the top shelf of the closet and threw it across her arm with the jeans. The jeans would be snug and the shirt would swallow her, but they were clean.

She took one step and stopped dead in her tracks. A noise, loud and cracking, resounded through the house like a bomb. The clothes dropped from her hands as her mind raced with imagined fears. She waited, but there was nothing but silence.

It was only a door slamming, Melissa told herself, determined to assuage her fears. She struggled for control. No more than the wind blowing through the cracks in the old house.

She stared out the window. The leaves on the giant cypress were motionless.

Her breath rose up to choke her, and she reached for the gun, cradling it in her hand like a lost friend. She tiptoed to the door and started down the narrow hallway. There was someone in the house, all right. The footsteps were slow and heavy.

She'd been so sure they'd be safe here. The cabin was isolated, and she was certain she'd have noticed lights if there had been another car on the dirt road that led through the swamp. But she'd been wrong. Someone must have followed them.

She listened, gun in hand, the adrenaline surging through her with hurricane force. The sounds were coming from the kitchen. And there was only one path from her to the kitchen and whoever waited there.

Her hands began to shake. She had the gun, but she'd never really planned to use it. Now she might not have a choice. She crept down the hall, her back against the wall.

Melissa raised the gun in front of her. One more step. She paused and listened.

A pot rattled against the gas range.

"Now where they go and hide that iron skillet?"

A voice, melodic and familiar, echoed down the empty hall. The tenseness melted, leaving Melissa weak. And thankful. She breathed deeply and stepped into the kitchen.

"And just what might you be needing with an iron skillet?" she questioned happily, crossing the floor and heading straight for the open arms of Cotile.

"*Mon Dieu*, cher. You finally got yourself down to old Bayou Lachere. Thought you'd just up and forgot your old aunt Cotile." She laughed, her thick Cajun accent filling the room.

Melissa felt Cotile's arms around her, loving and warm. She swallowed a tear. She'd come home.

"Goodness, child, what you got yourself?" Cotile took the heavy Smith and Wesson and turned it over in her hand, examining it carefully. "What you planned to shoot with a big old .38?" She rubbed her hands across the smooth metal. "Not a nutria, and that's for sure."

Melissa stared at the pistol. "I don't know."

Cotile tried to hand it to her, but she pushed it away. Twice in the last few minutes she'd aimed the gun. Once while asleep, once while awake. Either time, pulling the trigger would have been a mistake, a deadly mistake. "I never plan to carry one again."

"You in some kind of trouble, cher?" Cotile eyed her suspiciously as she waited for an answer.

It would be useless to lie. The old dear was far too astute. She'd see right through it. She always had. Yet how much should she tell her? It was one thing to make decisions that put herself in danger. It was quite another to involve an innocent neighbor.

"No, no trouble." She opted for the lie. "I'm just trying to avoid a bunch of hungry reporters out to devour more of the Rocky Matherne story. I don't blame them, of course. I've hounded my share of sources, too, and I'm sure I will again. But, right now, I just need a quiet place to grab a little R and R."

"That man with you, he need more than just a little rest. You just sit yourself down on that chair right there and tell me the truth while I cook up some venison sausage and some hot *pain perdu.*"

"You don't need to do that, really."

"*Mais,* cher, I already got it started. You need to eat, and your friend, he need to eat, too. And I need to just get me busy cooking for somebody else. You all too skinny. Cotile may be too fat, but you all be too skinny, for sure."

Melissa sank onto a kitchen chair. Arguing with Cotile would be a waste of strength, and she didn't have enough to waste.

Besides, Cotile was right. It had been almost twenty-four hours since the hurried meal at the truck stop. They needed food. And memories of waking up to the smell of French bread dipped in fresh eggs and milk sizzling in an old cast iron skillet were doing strange things to her stomach and making her mouth water.

She leaned back and listened to Cotile's easy chatter, comforted by the musical cadence of her speech. It was a relief to talk to someone she could trust completely. Cotile wasn't actually family, but she was close enough. She'd been Gramme's best friend for as long as Melissa could remember, and she'd always thought of her as a favorite aunt.

"How did you know we were here?" she questioned.

"I saw the blue Ford out on the road. I said, I don't know who that could be for. So I said to myself, Cotile, you better get yourself over there and find out what's going on."

"Oh, my God! You mean I left the door unlocked? Anyone could've just walked in during the night."

"You left it unlocked, all right, child, but it wouldn't have mattered none if you'd double bolted it. A person could've broken the door right down and you wouldn't have heard 'em. I banged on the door for ten minutes or more myself 'fore I just stuck my head in."

"I know I was tired, but... What time was that?"

"Around eight o'clock. Well after sunup. That's when I heard all that moaning and groaning. Wouldn't be much of a neighbor if I just stayed away with somebody suffering like that, now would I?"

"So that's where the quilt came from, and the water."

Melissa leaned back, watching Cotile's wrinkled hands measure the coffee grounds and pour them into the stove-top coffeemaker.

"The guy in there." The old woman broke into her thoughts, determined to hear the whole story. "How'd he get hurt?"

"Someone tried to kill me. He saved my life."

Cotile spun around on her heels. "That dirty Rocky Matherne! I talk to Old Joe from the store just yesterday. He was down here trying to kill himself a duck or two. He told me that fat loudmouth was all over the TV spouting off that big mouth of his about how you set him up. Might have known he'd have one of his boys try something."

She tore off a portion of ground sausage and pounded it into a pattie. "What the deputy said? They find that crazy man yet?"

"No." This time Melissa didn't lie. She just avoided mentioning they hadn't even called the police. "We're not sure this was Rocky's doings, although there's good reason to suspect he's behind it."

"Of course, he done it. Why, who else would want you dead? A pretty little thing like you. And your Gramme always said you sweet like sugarcane."

Who else wanted her dead? That was not an easy question for an investigative reporter. For every wrongdoing she exposed, someone had to pay. She didn't even try to keep track of all the threats she received.

Still, there was a vast difference between making idle threats and attempting to blow someone into tiny pieces. A person would have to be obsessed with hatred or revenge to pull that off. Or just plain crazy.

She shivered as images of Brett broke into her thoughts. Brett holding a gun and forcing her to drive. Brett shaking uncontrollably. But now it was Brett, injured and weak from saving her life. She leaned her elbows on the table for support and fought the waves of nausea that washed over her.

She had to stop going over what had happened and deal with the here and now. "Cotile, I need to find a doctor for Brett. You know everyone around here. Who's the most likely to make a house call and then keep his mouth shut?"

"Can't get nobody to make a house call out here anymore, not since old Doc Gonzales died. All them young doctors move into Lafayette or New Iberia, my nephew included. He set himself up in town in one of them fancy offices. If you need doctoring, you go to them now."

Melissa had expected as much.

"That fellow in there, he told me himself, he don't want no doctors passing by here," Cotile continued. "And he 'bout as determined as a hungry 'gator. You just might as well believe him, cher. What he said, he means, or I don't know my 'gators."

"He told you that? When?"

"This morning. He told me a lot of things, though I don't know how much stock I'd put in his ramblings. But he was sure clear about nobody knowing he was here. He's not going to a doctor, and he don't want one come by here. Not a doctor and nobody else!"

"He's got to have a tetanus shot. And something to ward off an infection."

Cotile took a couple of mugs from the cupboard and filled them with hot coffee. She passed one to Melissa. "He's a grown man, cher. He's not so sick he can't take care of his own self. Besides, I promised I'd help him. I know a thing or two about doctoring, myself. I been take care of sick folk around here since 'fore you was born."

"You promised? Why would you do such a thing? You don't even know Brett."

"He need help." Cotile walked over to the table, drying her hands on a checkered dish towel. "I don't know what happened, Melissa, and maybe I don't need to know. But me, I never saw somebody who don't want to see a doctor like that. There's only one reason, cher. He's in trouble. Bad trouble!"

"You're right. Believe me, Cotile, I didn't mean to drag you into this. I was just looking for a place to come where we could be safe for a few days. I needed time to think, time to find some answers."

"You didn't drag me in, child. I'm just a nosy old neighbor, and I jumped in all by myself. If he a friend of yours, that's good enough for me."

Melissa reached out, wrapping her arms around the old woman's massive waist. "Thanks," she murmured softly.

"No need to thank me. What I'd be worth if I didn't help, huh? But..." She pulled up a chair and sat down, taking both of Melissa's hands in her own.

Melissa waited silently, not sure she wanted to hear what was to come, knowing she had no choice.

"I know you young folks don't take stock in superstitions, but I know what I'm talking about. That man in there, he a strong man. Powerful, but something more. Something from deep inside. I feel it, sure as I feel your hands in mine. I'm not saying it's bad, I'm just telling you the way it is, for your own good. He gonna get his way. Nothing can stop him but the grave."

Melissa didn't want to hear more, but she waited silently, her hands still clasped with Cotile's.

"Be careful, cher. Just be careful."

THE SUN BEAT DOWN on the road mercilessly, and Melissa made a mental note to add sunglasses to her ever-growing list of necessities. She hadn't wanted to drive into town today, but there were so many things they needed. Everything she'd brought with her from New Orleans had blown up with the car. Besides, she needed to let her brother know she was safe. If he'd heard about her car, he'd be frantic.

She glanced at her rearview mirror. An old gray van rode her tail for a minute or two, then passed her and sped out of sight. Good. She had to be careful. It wasn't wise, she knew, driving the blue Ford, but it was all she had. Cotile had a pickup, an old '68 that had been on its last legs for years, but it wasn't running now. It had quit on her two weeks ago, and she hadn't bothered to get it repaired. "Nowhere to go anyway," she'd explained.

Melissa had mentioned going into town at breakfast, but Brett had gotten so upset, she'd let it ride. He was determined not to let her out of his sight. For her protection, he'd argued, but Melissa was sure he was worried about his skin, as well. He knew one call from her, and he'd be picked up by the state police and whizzed to the hospital.

But she had no intention of making that call. At least not yet. There were still too many unanswered questions.

She'd hung around the house all morning, keeping a wary eye on Brett. But there was nothing to watch. He'd stayed in the bedroom, not talking at all, just poring over a stack of letters as if he were expecting the words to change before his eyes.

About one o'clock Cotile had returned, bringing a pot of seafood gumbo and a huge bowl of steamed rice. Brett had eaten like it was his last meal, singing Cotile's praises between every mouthful. He hadn't lasted long after that, falling fast asleep in the big bed, one of the letters still clutched in his hand.

Melissa moved her neck from side to side. She could have used a nap herself. She stretched as much as the steering wheel would allow. Gramme's bed would feel awfully good tonight.

She noted the speedometer, then eased her foot from the accelerator pedal. As much as she'd like to get her business finished and get back to the safety of the cabin, it would be dangerous to push the speed limit. The last thing she wanted right now was an encounter with a state trooper. One quick check would alert the authorities to her whereabouts. If Brett was right and the owner of the blue Ford really was tied in with the police in some way, Melissa would be a sitting duck for his next attack.

She pushed the thought from her mind. She was being careful. She'd take care of business close to home today. Tomorrow or the next day, she'd drive into Lafayette and desert the Ford. Luckily she still had her purse with her identification and credit cards. She'd have no trouble renting a car.

She drove on, trying to concentrate on the passing scenery. She'd often traveled to the cabin with her family before Gramme's death, but her father and older brother had always taken the Interstate as far as they could, avoiding the narrow bridges and slower back-woods roads.

In the process, they'd also avoided a lot of local color, Melissa decided. Her favorites were the two-pump gas and grocery stores that advertised cold beer and hot boudin. She'd stopped at one, not for the spicy Cajun sausage, but just to use the phone.

She'd changed her mind, however, once she'd noted the group of elderly men gathered near the outdoor pay phone. They were merely exchanging man talk and chewing their tobacco, but she had no doubt they'd be willing to stop their chatting long enough to listen in on a stranger's conversation. So she opted for a cold cola instead, the diet variety now that Cotile was doing the cooking, and climbed into the Ford.

A road sign came into view, and Melissa squinted, blocking out some of the sun's bright rays in order to make out the numbers. Only five more miles to Abbe-ville. She'd be able to pick up a few of the supplies they needed there. Toothbrushes and a razor for Brett were at the top of the list.

And a change of clothes for her and a pair of men's jeans if she could find them. Weak as he was, Brett had managed to shower and change into some of her broth-er's hunting garb. The shirts had fit fairly well, just a little snug through the shoulders. And the pants weren't too long. It was just that they gathered around his waist like a woman's skirt.

Her brother was a huge man, large and booming, overpowering everyone around him. Brett had to be just as tall and just as broad through the shoulders, but his body was muscle where Cody's was fat.

And Brett dominated with a different type of authority, a powerful force that spoke even when his voice was silent. Every time she was near him, she felt it.

Her face reddened at her thoughts. She couldn't explain her attraction to him, but neither could she deny it. It was as if virility surged through his veins, never letting her forget that he was all man.

A man to be careful of. That's what Cotile had warned. But even she was falling under his spell. She'd been eager to stay with him today. But would she have been so eager if she knew the truth about how he'd come to be in Melissa's life, if she knew who he really was?

Not that Melissa knew who he was. She only knew where he'd been. At least, where he'd been recently. A hospital where the patients slept behind locked doors. A place he had no intention of returning to. Not while he had breath left to fight it.

Melissa slowed the car as she entered town, watching for signs to lead her to the best place to pick up the items on her list. It shouldn't take long. She only needed a few days' supplies. After that, Brett should be able to strike out on his own. He'd be out of her life as quickly as he'd dropped in.

And she'd be free to go home and take care of pressing business. Number one would be to call the police and the insurance company to report her car's demise.

"And when did you first suspect the car was missing?" She could hear their questions now. And she could see the expressions on their faces when she gave them the answer. "About a split second after I watched it blast across the night sky."

IT WAS ALMOST FOUR when Melissa locked her purchases in the trunk of the car and walked into the coffee shop. She'd managed to pick up everything in only two stops.

And her luck had held. Not one person had recognized her as the well publicized target of Rocky's wrath. Evidently small town folks didn't expect to run into celebrities, even dubious ones, in their local establishments.

She ordered a cup of coffee and then rummaged through her billfold for her calling card. Her brother was all the immediate family she had left since her parents' death, and he took his role as older brother much too seriously. He had a hard time realizing his little sister was twenty-seven years old and able to take care of herself.

The phone was answered on the first ring. "Mr. Bentley's office. May I help you?"

"Hi, Susie. This is Melissa. Is Cody in?"

"Melissa. Where are you? Mr. Bentley's been worried sick."

Melissa grimaced. She didn't have the patience for a conversation with Cody's know-it-all, tell-it-all secretary. "I'm fine," she responded nonchalantly, dismissing Susie's excited inquisition. "Is Cody around?"

"He's with a client right now. Dr. Abramson, you know, the one who's involved in the big swindling case."

No. Melissa didn't know and she didn't care. "Well, look, Susie, just tell him I called, and that I'm fine. I'm going to stay out of town until things blow over."

"I don't blame you. Your story was on the front page of the paper yesterday. Everybody's talking about you.

Not all good, of course. Rocky's supporters are out for your hide.''

"It'll blow over in a day or two. Soon as a new story comes along.''

"Maybe, but I'd hate to be in your shoes right now. You better leave me a number where Mr. Bentley can reach you. He's pretty upset with your just leaving town that way without telling him where you were going. Reporters are calling here all the time asking us, and we don't know what to tell them.''

But if she knew, she'd tell. There was no doubt about that. "Just keep putting them off. Eventually, they'll get tired and leave you alone.''

"And that nice young detective you dated for a while called, too. You know, Marvin Brady. He sounded awfully upset. I tell you, girl, I just don't understand why you didn't hang on to that one. The guy is solid hunk.''

"What can I say, Susie? Guess I have no taste. Listen, I've got to run. Just tell Cody I'll get back to him in a few days.''

"Melissa, wait, you can't just hang up without telling us—''

Melissa returned the phone to the cradle, one chore out of the way.

Her mind whirled with possibilities. Evidently Cody hadn't heard about her car. But someone had to have investigated it by now. Of course, there was the unlikely possibility that neither the serial number nor any of her identifying possessions had been found in one piece. Or there was the much more likely scenario that someone was covering it up.

Her hands grew clammy. The chances were darn good that whoever had tried to do her in was not working alone. Brett's story about the mad bomber being connected to the police was suddenly a lot more credible. And driving the blue Ford was a lot more dangerous.

She took a deep breath and reached into her purse, this time pulling out a black book of phone numbers. There was nothing she could do about the car now, but there was something she could do about her other problems. She dialed the number of the records room of the New Orleans Police Department. The phone rang once, then again. Her pulse raced, and her fingers began to shake.

She placed the phone in the cradle.

One call was probably all it would take. A routine check of police reports for Tuesday, November seventh, and she'd at least know who Brett was. With a little luck, she might find out a whole lot more.

So why had she hung up the phone? What was she afraid to learn? That he was an escaped mental patient? She already knew that. That he was dangerous? Dangerous enough to take her hostage at the point of a gun? She knew that, too.

It was strange, though. She couldn't begin to understand it, but it was as if there was some unspoken bond between them. She'd heard of that before. How saving someone's life brought you close. In some cultures, you even belonged to the person.

She picked up the phone again and dialed. The trauma of the last few days was getting to her. She didn't belong to Brett. Not in any way. There was no reason for her to fear the truth.

"Records room. Marion Olson here. How can I help you?"

Good. It was Marion. One of the friendly ones who didn't despise reporters. At least not all of them. "Hi, Marion. This is Melissa Bentley. I just need a little in-

formation about some guy who escaped from a mental
hospital, early Tuesday, I believe. Let's see, I have my
notes here somewhere. Yes, here it is. Brett something
or other. I can't quite make out the last name.''

"Melissa Bentley! I didn't expect to hear from you.
Girl, you're sure the talk of the town. Not to mention
what they're saying about you around the station.
Where in the world are you? Those TV guys are saying
you just up and disappeared.''

"Good. I'm hoping it stays that way. In fact, I'd really appreciate it if you'd keep this conversation under
your hat.''

"Sure thing, Miss Bentley. You don't have to worry
about me. I can keep a secret good as the next one.''

That was exactly why Melissa *was* worried, but she
needed Marion's help. "Do you have anything on this
Brett whatever his name is?'' She kept her tone light.

"Samson. Brett Samson. The girls in the office were
talking about it. You know, he's one of those Samsons
from up around Baton Rouge. They own that big plantation, Samson Place. Hold on a minute. I'll pull up the
records on it if I can get this computer to work right. It
was down most of the morning.''

Melissa waited. Samson Place. The name sounded
vaguely familiar.

"Here it is, but it's pretty sketchy. Dr. Stuart Mosher
from Magnolia Heights called the police about ten
o'clock Tuesday morning and reported a missing patient. Said he'd attacked a nurse and took her keys.
Wait, there's more. A known drug addict with a history of violence. They're anxious to have him found and
returned to the hospital, but for some reason they want
his escape kept quiet. Probably because he's got money.
That's what counts in this town. Money.''

Melissa scribbled the information in her notebook and thanked Marion for her help, being sure to take the time to ask about her two kids. It paid to keep on people's good sides. Not that Marion had given her anything confidential, but still, you never knew what you might need next time.

She skimmed her notes. Escape reported at ten in the morning. But he had to have left hours before that. It was ten-thirty when she'd arrived at the truck stop, and he'd covered more than a hundred and fifty miles by then.

She ran her pen down the quickly scribbled notes. A druggie and dangerous. Nothing there to substantiate Brett's stories. She started to her table, but stopped mid stride. Nothing there to contradict them, either.

She rang information and asked for the number of Magnolia Heights. She dialed quickly, before she changed her mind. She was already in deep. She might as well go all the way.

Chapter Six

The aroma of Cajun spices hung heavy in the air as Melissa pushed through the kitchen door. She stepped inside and stood quietly as her eyes adjusted to the darkness. The sun had just taken its final plunge below the horizon, and bands of coppery hues still lightened the night sky. Inside, behind the drawn curtains, shades of dark gray met her gaze.

"Brett." Melissa called his name softly. Only silence returned her greeting. She flipped on the light, erasing the shadows. "Brett, it's me, Melissa."

She glanced around the kitchen. There were no traces of the spicy lunch she'd shared earlier with Brett and Cotile. The dishes had been washed and put away and the counter wiped clean. Nothing but the pungent odors remained to reassure her that her memory was not playing tricks on her.

She walked down the narrow hallway, peeking into each room for any sign of Brett, but everything was just as they had found it last night. Even the bed he'd slept in had been smoothed over with the faded chenille spread.

"Brett!" She called his name again, this time louder, her anxiety no longer masked. Perhaps he'd wakened to find her gone and just set out through the woods on his own. She breathed deeply, amazed at the wave of concern that washed over her. It didn't last long. Panic followed close behind.

Maybe he hadn't just walked out on his own. Maybe someone had followed them here last night. No, that wasn't likely. If someone had known of their whereabouts, he would never have waited until this afternoon to make his presence known. Besides, the only one who could have followed them was the psycho who'd rigged the bomb to her car. And he wouldn't have been looking for Brett. He was out to get her.

Melissa walked through the house and into the yard. The sky had darkened, and she wrapped her arms around her, warding off the early evening chill. An old bullfrog croaked in the distance, and a chorus of a thousand tree frogs responded to his call. Melissa stood quietly, letting the bayou night envelop her as she tried to make sense of Brett's disappearance.

Something moved, rustling in the grass behind her. Instinctively she reached in her pocket for the gun. But it was no longer there. It was high atop the closet in her bedroom where she'd placed it after the morning's experiences.

"Are you alone?"

The familiar deep voice jolted her into control. She whirled to face Brett. "Obviously not. Not now that you've quit playing your little game of hide-and-seek."

"Game, Melissa? I'd hardly call fighting for one's life a game, although you seem to think of it as one." He reached out and clutched her shoulder, his strength piercing the soft fleece of the sweatshirt. "Where have you been?" he demanded.

"Out. To get some things we needed. And I don't need you to tell me what's safe." She jerked away from his grasp. "I'm back, aren't I?"

"This time. But I don't relish having to save your life on a daily basis just because you're so damn sure of yourself that you can't take a few normal precautions." He started to walk toward the house, but stopped, turning to face her. "I'm sorry. It's just that I was so damn worried about you."

His words of concern sounded good, but they didn't ring totally true. Concern for her might explain his anger, but it didn't explain why he'd made the house look as if they'd never been here or why he'd hidden in the surrounding woods when he'd heard her approach.

"Who are you trying to kid, Brett? It's your own skin you're worried about."

"I'm no fool, Melissa. Besides, I didn't know if you'd be coming back at all. And if you didn't, I wasn't taking a chance on someone else finding out that I'd been here. And I sure couldn't chance your returning with someone to carry me back to the hospital."

He stepped closer. The lines in his brow deepened, his dark eyes mirroring the desperateness of his plight. He took a handkerchief from his pocket and wiped his face. It was dotted with beads of perspiration in spite of the coolness of the night.

"I can't go back. I can't sit there and rot in that prison they call a hospital while my brother's murderer goes free."

Melissa studied his face. "You saved my life. I owe you one. I won't turn you in. I told you that, and I always keep my word." She met his gaze and found a touch of warmth. "Unless I have very good reasons not to," she added cautiously.

Brett took her hands in his and caressed them gently. She wanted to pull away again, but not for the same reasons as before. His effect on her was frightening, awakening feelings she'd buried three years ago. Feelings that could only cloud her judgment when her very survival depended on rational thinking.

"But," he whispered, pulling her closer, "I wasn't only worried about myself. It's suicide for you to venture out in that blue Ford, and you know it."

"Let's just drop the subject for now. I have groceries to put away." She started toward the car.

Brett walked ahead of her. "I'll get those." He swooped up most of the packages with one hand. "Looks like you bought out the store. It will take us weeks to eat all this food."

"Then we definitely won't be eating all of it," she quipped, grabbing the last package.

Once inside, Melissa busied herself with putting away the groceries while Brett dug through the packages. He stopped when he came across the razor. Rubbing his hands across the stubble of dark hairs that dotted his chin, he smiled sheepishly. "Guess the lady doesn't like the rugged look."

Melissa felt the color rise to her cheeks and prayed her thoughts were not as transparent as they felt. His rugged features, the intensity evident in his every action, the raw sensuality emanating from his very being, were as constant and as real as the air they breathed. Whiskers or not, her attraction to him wasn't likely to abate anytime soon. And heaven help her if it grew much stronger.

"I just thought you might be more comfortable after a shave." Rising to her tiptoes, she tried to slide a sack of flour onto the top shelf.

"Here, let me help you with that." He moved behind her, his hard body leaning into hers as he pushed the flour to the back of the shelf.

His rough hand brushed against hers, and he held it there. For an eternity. She barely breathed, the feel of him numbing her brain and melting her resolve.

He placed his hands on the counter, one on either side of her, encircling her, yet not touching. She spun to face him and gazed into his eyes, into smoky depths of smoldering desire. They held her, pulling her to him with a silent, mesmerizing force.

He lifted his hand to her face and cupped it around her chin, his thumb tracing the lines of her lower lip. Her pulse raced, and her head grew dizzy.

He wrapped his arm around her waist and pulled her closer, and she could feel his muscles tighten, sense a determination that she couldn't understand. Then, without warning, he stiffened and pushed her away.

Melissa stared into his eyes, but the dark pools had become hard steel, the passion dying as quickly as it had been born.

He turned away from her stare and stepped toward the table, tightly clutching the back of one of the chairs. "I'm sorry, Melissa."

"There's no reason to be." She forced a calm into her voice. "Nothing happened. No harm done." It was amazing how easy the white lies came once you began. And it was true, at least in part. If he could pull away so easily, apparently no harm had been done to him.

"That's not what I meant."

"No? Then what did you mean?" Melissa saw the shrug of his shoulders, but she couldn't read his expression. He kept his back to her, his fingers still wrapped tightly around the chair.

"It doesn't matter. It won't happen again. Not here. Not like this."

"Brett, I think it's time we talk, really talk. You said a few things the other night, after the explosion, something about your sister-in-law."

"Ah, yes. Dear Sylvia." He spit the name out contemptuously. "I said she killed my brother. She's walking around free now, playing the role of bereaved widow, but she's going to pay. I'll see that she pays if it's the last thing I ever do."

Melissa shivered at the fierceness of his words, knowing they were much more than idle threats. "Do you have proof?"

"Not yet, but I will. The proof is in the letters. It has to be hidden there somewhere."

"Hidden? I don't understand."

"The letters are all jumbled, as if Jason had just rambled on without rhyme or reason. Like a man half out of his mind. Like I've been for the past three and a half weeks. Locked away in some nuthouse with no way of finding the diary. But not at all like Jason's usually meticulous correspondence."

"Letters, a diary, hospitals. You're not making a lot of sense, either, Brett. If you want my help, you'll have to start at the beginning."

"Want your help?" His voice rose. "You've got things all wrong, lady."

"Is that it? We're back to lady again?" A few moments ago they'd shared an intimacy so compelling that Melissa was still shaken, but for Brett it was back to lady again as soon as she suggested he let her in on the events that were ruling his life.

He sat down in one of the chairs. "I told you. This is nasty business. There's no reason for you to get involved. It's bad enough you have some lunatic trying to kill you, and you running off in his car, risking your life for... for a few lousy groceries and a razor.''

"I didn't risk my life. I was careful, and I didn't go far. We're miles from where the explosion occurred. Besides, the man's probably come down off his high by now and is laid up somewhere hoping we don't catch up with him.''

"You don't believe that any more than I do." Brett reached for her hands and coaxed her into the chair beside his. "That attack was well planned by someone, or several someones, who knew exactly what they were doing. You won't be safe until they're caught or dead.''

"So here we are, you with a vendetta, me with a stalker. We're in this thing together, whether you like it or not. You might as well tell me your whole story." Melissa walked over to the stove and picked up the coffeepot. "Starting with the letters.''

"I'll tell you about them, Melissa. But I mean what I say. You are not to get involved. Sylvia's already committed one murder. She won't hesitate to do it again, not if her life of luxury is threatened.''

"Don't worry. Like you said, I have enough trouble of my own." Melissa carefully avoided making promises that she had no intention of keeping.

He tipped his chair back and stared off into space. "Okay, the letters. What do you want to know? They're from Jason, my brother, my *late* brother." His voice grew heavy, the sadness of his loss evident in every word. "The first one was dated September eighth, a little more than a month before his death. It didn't say much, just that he'd been sick for a few weeks, some kind of flu, and that he couldn't seem to get his strength back.''

Melissa put the pot over a low flame and settled beside Brett. "What did you do when you got the letter?"

"Nothing." He hammered his fist against the wooden table. "Absolutely nothing. If I had, Jason might be alive today. I tried to call, but Sylvia said he was feeling much better, that he'd gone out for a while. I left that day on a three-week excursion, not dreaming the greedy gold digger was planning his death even then."

"So he wrote again?" Melissa urged him on.

"Yeah, six times in all, though I didn't see the other five until I returned. He wrote about roses and dogs, generals and fountains. There was no pattern to his letters, and nothing to indicate he feared for his life. But in every one of them he made some mention of a diary. 'Life is no more than buried secrets locked in a hidden diary.' He wrote that twice. Or at least something to that effect."

"Did you try to reach him again?"

"I called him the day I returned and for the next two days after that. But there was no answer, nothing but that damn... that irritating answering machine saying leave a message. They travel a lot, always have, and to tell you the truth, I didn't think much more about it."

"And no one returned your calls?"

"Oh, yes, Sylvia finally found time to talk to me." His voice grew harsh. "Just a friendly call to tell me that her husband had passed away. A sudden and massive heart attack, she said. We were just lucky he didn't have to suffer."

The tremor returned to Brett's hands, and his shoulders slumped, his usually tense body growing limp. "But it wasn't a heart attack that killed my brother. It was a heartless . . ." His voice broke and he buried his head in his hands.

Melissa eased her arm around his shoulder, her sympathy genuine. She knew what it was to lose family. The sudden death of her parents still haunted her. She squeezed lightly on his shoulder. He flinched and pulled away.

"Sorry. I didn't think about your injuries. Your shoulder must still be awfully sore. Why don't you try to get some rest?"

Brett lifted his head. He stared into Melissa's eyes, and she looked away, afraid for him to read her thoughts, afraid to even acknowledge them herself. He reached over and took a lock of her hair, curling it around his finger. "You're a very special woman, Melissa."

She waited, the silence enveloping them like thick bayou fog. He leaned toward her, his lips only inches away. Girding all the resolve she could muster, she pulled away. Another time, another place, maybe things could have been different between them. But not now. Brett had his reasons. And she had hers.

"Are you hungry, Brett? I bought some canned soup. Not nearly as good as Cotile's gumbo, of course."

"No. Not now. But you're right. About my needing rest. I slept nearly half of the afternoon, but the fatigue won't go away."

"Why don't you get ready for bed?" she suggested, her weariness bearing down now that she'd reached the safety of the cabin. "I'll get the first-aid supplies and be with you in a minute."

Brett rose from his chair slowly. "Thanks, but that's not necessary. Cotile took care of everything. She's quite a nurse. Knows more about medicine than most doctors.''

"And if half the tales she spins are true, she's had more experience than some," Melissa answered. She took a coffee mug from the shelf and poured it full of the strong brew. She'd be up late tonight. Her mind was far too full to sleep.

"Yeah. These people along the bayou seem to take care of themselves without much help from outsiders. You have to admire them for that." Brett turned to walk toward the door. "And they're not afraid to stick their necks out for someone else," he added.

"That's true," Melissa answered, without looking up from her mug of black liquid, "but they're not too proud to take help when they need it."

"And you think I am, Melissa?"

"I think we both are," she answered truthfully.

"Maybe you're right," he answered.

He stopped at the door and lounged against it, fatigue beginning to show in the slump of his shoulders.

"You just need some rest, Brett. We'll talk again, in the morning."

"Right. In the morning. But if you need anything during the night, anything at all, just call, and I'll be there."

Melissa watched silently as he turned and rounded the corner leading into the hallway. His words were comforting. Her view wasn't. A large stain covered the back of his shirt where she'd touched his shoulder just minutes earlier. Apparently his wounds were not healing as well as he'd have her believe.

She sipped her coffee. The bayou offered a temporary haven, but their problems were far from over. Infection still posed a serious threat, and even though she'd had a busy day, she hadn't gotten far in finding out who had unsuccessfully plotted her untimely demise.

Even her attempts to find out about the mysterious Brett Samson had been practically futile. She'd learned almost nothing, except for his last name.

But that could all change tomorrow. She'd drive into town, ditch the Ford and keep her appointment with Dr. Mosher. Brett would never consent to her going, but she didn't need his permission. She'd get up early and leave while he slept. He wouldn't have the chance to stop her.

THE SECRETARY tapped her well-manicured nails on the table and motioned for Melissa to have a seat, the phone receiver balanced rather precariously between her chin and right shoulder. Melissa slipped into one of the uncomfortable chairs, keeping her raincoat wrapped around her. She had on the jeans and crisp cotton shirt she'd purchased in Abbeville yesterday, but they seemed out of place in the sleek, modern office.

And she was not here to call attention to herself. She was here to get the facts. She'd worked on her story during the three-hour drive into New Orleans, and she had it down pat.

She was a close friend of Brett's dead brother, although they'd drifted apart in recent years. She didn't know Brett well. In fact, she'd only met him once, several years ago, but she'd heard he was not doing well and she wanted to do whatever she could to help him. As a favor to Jason. She was sure he'd have done as much for her if their situations had been reversed.

It should work. There was no reason for it not to unless Dr. Mosher knew a lot about Jason. Unless he knew enough that he could ask her the type of questions that would prove her own story false. She doubted that he did. Magnolia Heights was a large institution, and judging from the luxurious looks of his reception area, Dr. Mosher was probably the top gun.

She'd be surprised if the good doctor knew much about any of his patients. Even ones as wealthy as Jason and Brett. And there was little risk of his recognizing her even though her name had apparently been in the news often these last few days. Reporters rated mention, but not pictures. Those were reserved for the truly newsworthy or socially prominent, and neither group included her.

"Miss Jackson, the doctor will see you now. *Miss Jackson.*"

Melissa jumped, finally aware that she was being addressed. That was the problem with giving fake names. You forgot them yourself. She stood up and followed the shapely secretary through a large door and into Dr. Mosher's office.

"Come in, Miss Jackson."

The doctor's voice was smooth as velvet, and his large hand covered hers in a friendly handshake.

"May I help you with your coat?"

"No, thank you. I've got a bit of a chill. I'll just wear it for a while."

"Very well." He gestured toward a pillowed sofa, upholstered in a deep green. "Won't you have a seat?"

Melissa opted for a chair nearer the doctor's large, polished desk, the focal point of an impressive room. Bookshelves filled with thick volumes carrying impressive titles lined the paneled walls, and framed prints of pastoral scenes were interspersed with hanging diplomas and various awards.

The doctor took a seat behind the desk. He smiled broadly, showing a set of perfect white teeth. He must have been at least fifty, but he had thick salt-and-pepper hair and a natural charm that was timeless.

He leaned toward her, his eyes taking in every detail. "It's a lovely day outside, but quite chilly for New Orleans, even in November."

Melissa agreed and waited, sure the doctor was not going to waste his expensive time on small talk. He didn't disappoint her.

"And how may I be of service to you, Miss Jackson?"

"As I mentioned on the telephone yesterday, I'm a friend of Brett Samson's. Well, actually I was a friend of his brother Jason."

Mosher leaned back in his chair. "I see. His death must have been a painful shock for you."

He spoke with a compelling compassion that put her at instant ease. But he was a professional, she reminded herself, trained to manipulate, to control the mind and the subconscious. She'd have to be careful or she'd forget her agenda, falling under his spell like his patients probably did. At least some of his patients.

"Yes, it was a shock, but that's not why I'm here. I came to ask about Brett Samson." Melissa weighed her words carefully. "Jason helped me out a few years ago when I needed a friend. I never had the opportunity to repay him. Now that he's gone..." Melissa dropped her lids and her voice, adopting a proper tone of sadness. "Well, I'd like to repay him by helping his brother."

"That's a very worthy sentiment. And I wish I could help you. Unfortunately, I'm not at liberty to discuss my patients with anyone. A matter of ethics, you know." He studied her openly. "Just what exactly do you know about Brett Samson?"

Melissa considered her response. There was something about the man she didn't trust. Too polished. Too... She wasn't sure. It was nothing she could put her finger on. But still he came across as purely professional. The chances were slim that he'd give out any information at all. And if she didn't give him some reason to confide in her, they'd quickly drop to none.

"I know he escaped from this hospital. And..."

Mosher got out of his chair and walked over to stand in front of Melissa. He leaned against the desk. "And what, Miss Jackson?" His voice was strained, trying to mask the urgency of his question.

She decided to throw out her best bait. "And I've talked to him."

The complacent look of control never vanished from Mosher's face, but he leaned closer. Just maybe she'd hit the right chord.

"Miss Jackson, as I said, I'm not at liberty to discuss my patients' problems with you, but I must tell you that Brett is a very sick man. If you truly want to do something worthwhile in the memory of Jason, you'll help us return Brett to the hospital at once. It's the only way he can get the help he needs."

"I'm afraid Brett disagrees with you."

Mosher pushed away from the desk and paced the room. Beads of perspiration dotted his wrinkled brow, and he slipped the expensive suit jacket from his shoulders, draping it over the back of his chair.

Good. He was agitated now. She'd definitely hit the right chord. He stepped in front of her, less than a foot away, forcing her to look up at him.

"This is a psychiatric hospital, Miss Jackson. Our patients do not always know what is best for them. Mr. Samson was placed here by his sister-in-law. It was an act of faith on her part to make that decision."

"You have a strange way with words, Dr. Mosher. One doesn't usually think of it as an act of faith to have someone committed to an institution."

"Look around you, Miss Jackson." Mosher waved his hand toward the window, angry indignation ruffling his usually smooth voice. "This is not your typical institution. We give our patients the best care and treatment that money can buy. We have waiting lists of people begging for our unparalleled services."

"Sorry, I didn't mean my statement as an insult. But, nonetheless, Brett is not begging to return. And, frankly, I see no reason for him to. Other than withdrawal symptoms from the drugs you gave him, he seems perfectly capable of taking care of himself without your excellent care."

"Am I to understand that you know where he is?" His tone grew hard and demanding as his professional image took a nosedive.

"No. I merely talked to him. I haven't the faintest idea where he is." Melissa had no real reason to dislike Mosher and even less reason to doubt him. He was a respected doctor. A patient escaped, and it was his duty to see that the patient was returned for treatment. It was as simple as that.

Or was it?

Mosher had blown his cool, and she suspected that didn't happen too often. For some reason, Brett was a special patient, and she needed to know why. She'd told him she wouldn't report his whereabouts, and she wouldn't. Not without good reason. If Mosher had those reasons, she needed to hear them.

Mosher pulled out a chair next to Melissa's. He'd taken the last few seconds to get his act together, and he'd been successful. He was calm and collected, and totally unreadable.

He spread his hands across his knees, and Melissa couldn't help but notice the Rolex on his wrist and a gold band sporting three large diamonds that all but dwarfed a finger on his right hand. If those diamonds were real, psychiatry was certainly paying a lot better for Dr. Mosher than for other doctors in the profession, at least the ones she'd dealt with.

Obviously aware of her gaze, Mosher began to finger the ring. "One cannot always go by appearances, Miss Jackson. And this is true in the case of Brett Samson. He is a sick man, and that sickness often manifests itself in violence. I didn't want to tell you these things, but I feel I must."

He reached out and took one of her hands in his. She didn't pull away, but instead leaned closer, taking in his every word. This is what she came to hear.

"Mr. Samson suffers from acute paranoia. He is convinced that everyone is out to get him. Sometimes that paranoia stretches to include those around him. Absurd as it may seem, he claims his brother was murdered even though the death certificate clearly states that he died of natural causes."

"You've seen that report?"

Mosher patted her hand comfortingly. "Yes, I have. And I've studied Brett's case thoroughly. This manufacturing of stories is not new. In fact, it dates back to adolescence. He has even been known to carry out dangerously bizarre actions to convince others that someone wants to kill him ... or them.''

Melissa cringed at the doctor's words. Images from the last two days flooded her mind. The doctor was right about Brett's insisting that someone had murdered his brother. And she and Brett were living in an isolated cabin because he'd convinced her she was in imminent danger.

But her life *was* in danger. The explosion was real, and it had not been an accident. It was a violent act perpetrated by someone with a sick mind. Someone like ...

Melissa felt the shaking from its beginning, somewhere deep in the core of her being. It flowed slowly through her body, reducing her to a quivering mass of nerves.

Mosher eased closer and placed an arm around her, one hand still locked with hers, now clutching feverishly to his.

"I'm so sorry I had to frighten you like this, but there was no other way." His words were slow and soothing. "I fear you are falling under Brett's powers. You are just his type. Young and beautiful."

The doctor patted her comfortingly, like one might do a frightened child.

"You wouldn't be the first. He has a way with young women. He works on them, building up their sympathy, winning their trust. And then he turns on them, like he did with Sylvia." He shook his head disapprovingly, a look of concern settling over the chiseled features of his face.

Melissa breathed deeply, determined to regain some semblance of control. Emotions, especially fear, would blind her judgment.

"What happened?" Her mouth was dry as cotton, and her words came out as little more than a whisper. "What did he do to Sylvia?"

"Why, didn't you know? He tried to kill her."

Chapter Seven

Tried to kill her. Kill her. Kill her.

The words hammered in Melissa's brain as she raced down the dark stairwell. She could have taken the elevator, but her body needed the release of physical exercise, the unconscious sensation of running from truths she didn't want to face. Her breath came in ragged gasps, but she continued her pace, never slowing until she reached the first floor and pushed through the heavy door and out into the brisk air.

She leaned against the building, trying desperately to gain her composure. Somehow she had managed to hear Dr. Mosher out and then make at least a semigraceful exit while his words pummeled her fragile control. She took a deep breath. She had to gain her usual tenacious grip on reality.

She was in New Orleans and likely to be recognized on the busy street. Cautiously, she scanned her surroundings.

Only one person seemed to have noticed her appearance. A tall, well-dressed man a few yards away was walking slowly and staring at her, obviously aware of her heavy breathing. She smiled a silent acknowledgment that she was fine, and he hurried on his way.

She looked around again. Reasonably assured that no one was following her, she pulled her coat tighter and strode toward the rented car. Safely inside, she locked the doors and fastened the seat belt before pulling out into the noontime traffic. Her eyes were on the road, but her mind was frantically trying to make sense of the doctor's revelations.

Brett had fallen into a drug-enhanced state of paranoia, Dr. Mosher had explained, and he'd let his hallucinations dictate his actions. When the drugs took over, he might do anything, and frequently did. He wouldn't be able to stay off the drugs for long. Dr. Mosher had been adamant about that.

She didn't want to believe the doctor, but he was a licensed psychiatrist, in charge of an impressive hospital. What possible reason could he have to lie?

She pulled onto Interstate 10 and headed toward Metairie. The traffic was heavy. That was fine. Concentrating on it seemed to steady her nerves. She replayed the morning's meeting in her mind, weighing Mosher's descriptions against her images of Brett. It was impossible to reconcile his words with what she had seen with her own eyes.

Brett was a strong man with equally strong convictions. In desperate straits he might do almost anything. The kidnapping was ample proof of that. And he hated his sister-in-law for what he believed she had done to his brother. He had made that perfectly clear, too.

But his ruggedly handsome physique was not that of a man racked by drugs. He had been on them recently, but probably not for long. Even more important, he showed no interest in obtaining any sort of drugs now. Not even the ones he so desperately needed.

And he was no psychotic killer. Not unless all her intuitions were totally wrong. Her intuitions about the doctor as well as about Brett.

The doctor had been so smug in his assertions, as if he took some sadistic pleasure in letting Melissa know just how dangerous Brett was. And even his arm around her shoulder hadn't convinced her that he cared about her feelings. No, from the moment she'd met him, she'd felt as if he was manipulating the situation, and nothing had changed her mind about that.

He was used to being in charge of things, and he liked it that way. The only time he had let down his professional facade for even a moment was when he'd thought she might tell him where Brett was hiding.

He was determined to get Brett back in the hospital as soon as possible. But was his concern purely professional, or was there another reason he needed Brett back? Was Sylvia Samson paying big bucks to keep Brett locked away, to keep him away from evidence that proved she had killed her husband?

It was obvious from the doctor's statements that much of his information about Brett's past had come from Sylvia. That wasn't surprising. Melissa knew from experience that Brett was not one to go around spilling his guts to strangers. And judging from his determination not to return to the hospital, he certainly did not consider Dr. Mosher a friend.

Sylvia. She was the one who held the key to the puzzle, the one pulling all the strings. And, if she was half as devious as Brett insisted, she wouldn't bat an eye over accusing her brother-in-law of attempted murder and having him committed to a hospital.

But why a psychiatric hospital and not the jail? Mosher had said she'd chosen the hospital out of concern. But there could be other reasons. Melissa knew only too well how much proof it took to get a criminal conviction. She'd just spent countless hours doing that very thing, and even proving the guilt of a man as evil as Rocky had not been easy.

But getting a psychiatrist to buy the story of a well-respected citizen, that was different. It would be fairly easy to fool the doctor, have him lock Brett away long enough for Sylvia to find the diary herself. Find it and destroy all evidence against her.

So Melissa was back to square one. All the solid evidence pointed to Brett. Yet nothing contradicted his story. She could believe the doctor and a woman she'd never laid eyes on. Or she could believe Brett. If Mosher was right, she was hiding and abetting a psycho. More to the point, she was putting her life in danger, and she was already in enough with just Rocky's thugs to face.

If she believed Brett . . .

The confusion she'd come to know so intimately in the past two days settled once again in her mind and in her heart. Brett was an enigma. A man of mystery. A man of power. A man who'd forced his way into her life with brute strength and then awakened unexpected feelings of trust and tenderness.

Melissa slowed as an eighteen wheeler pulled in front of her. She glanced at the bright green sign announcing the causeway exit and then, as if automatically, she pulled into the far right lane.

Her apartment was less than a mile away. She'd decided not to stop there today, not to take the risk of running into a news reporter, or worse, one of Rocky's surprise visitors. But the lure was too great to resist. She longed for the cozy familiarity of her own four walls. And for time to think.

She didn't have to return to the cabin at all. She'd promised not to turn Brett in. She hadn't promised to baby-sit him. Besides, there was no guarantee Brett would still be at the cabin. He'd said he'd be out of her life as soon as he regained his strength. If that wasn't today, it would surely be tomorrow.

But she wasn't ready to go to the police just yet, wasn't ready to lay even the case of the exploding car into their bumbling hands. She had a little investigating of her own to do first.

She'd have to be careful, but that had become a way of life.

Melissa exited the interstate and then made several turns before pulling over to the curb. She had to make sure she wasn't being followed. The first car to pass was a red compact with two teenage girls. Not likely anyone to worry about. The driver chatted away without a look in her direction. Melissa breathed easier.

Several minutes passed before a gray van turned the corner, slowing down as it approached her. She watched it closely, her pulses racing as it slowed nearly to a stop. The driver was male, probably in his late twenties, and he turned and stared at her as he passed.

Her hands shook and her palms grew clammy as she turned the key, readying for a fast escape. He pulled into a driveway half a block down. But her imagination was working overtime, she decided, her pulse slowing to almost normal as a towheaded preschooler ran to greet the driver, hugging him and calling him daddy.

Melissa started the engine and pulled into the street that led behind her building. She eased between two larger cars and waited until the lot was almost empty before climbing out and hurrying toward her apartment.

Home free. The key turned easily and she pushed the door open. Open and into a new hell.

Her knees buckled. She reached out, clutching the doorframe for support. She longed to scream, to cry, to attack someone. She did nothing. Nothing but stand and stare at the chaos that surrounded her.

Her couch, her beautiful couch had been ripped to shreds, bits of the paisley cloth hanging limply above the cluttered carpet. And the picture, the one her mother had finished just before her death, lay on the floor, a sticky red substance clotting like blood against the painted roses.

She sank to the couch, her legs no longer able to support her heavy heart. She reached over and righted a table that had been overturned, its precious contents scattered like worthless debris. Paperweights, picture frames, crystal vases. All broken into tiny pieces, remnants of memories that should have lived forever.

Funny, no part of the room was left intact, yet Melissa saw each item, each piece of her life, separately. Each was an isolated part of the total destruction.

Tears burned her eyelids. She picked up what was left of a crystal candlestick, turning it over in her hands and then letting it slip from her fingers to fall to the floor.

Everything she owned had been destroyed in one sweep of a vicious man's hands. Vicious. Dangerous. And he'd been here, in her house. The private place where she ate, showered, slept.

Blood rushed to her head, and she pushed herself to her feet. The violent intruder could still be here. Somewhere hidden from view, silently waiting for her return.

She stood motionless, alert for the softest sound. But there was nothing. No breathing, no stirring. Willing her frozen feet to move, she tiptoed to the other side of the room and picked up a large piece of jagged glass.

Stealthily, she inched toward the bedroom door, to the only room of her compact apartment not visible from where she stood. The broken glass extended from her steady hand like a spear.

She hesitated at the door, her breath suspended in aching lungs. Then silently she pushed it open, praying to find an empty, untouched room, knowing she was asking the impossible.

She expected the worst, but nothing could have prepared her for the madman's atrocities. She gasped for breath, her body swaying forward, the room spinning like a carousel gone out of control. Her bones dissolved and the floor seemed to drop away beneath her feet. She lunged for the bed, grabbing the tall mahogany poster for support.

Her hands slipped in sticky blood. She stared at them in horror. No. Not blood. Paint that flowed thick and red like Brett's blood had the night of the explosion. Like hers would be doing if she'd been at home when her visitor had come.

The message was clear.

Her black negligee, once silky and sensual, lay spread across the bed, like a lady waiting for her lover. But the lover had turned violent. He'd plunged the shiny blade of a hunting knife through her heart.

Unable to stop herself, she ran her fingers across the lacy bodice that surrounded the would-be instrument of death. She touched her thumb to the sharp edge of the metal and then slowly guided her fingers up the cold blade.

Her heart constricted painfully, but she couldn't pull away. She sat immobile, staring at the circle of red that settled and spread across the black lace and onto the white satin of her pillow.

Something dripped from above her, splattering on the bed, striking her and staining her cotton shirt a deep crimson. She cringed and jumped to her feet.

Samson. The paint had come from Samson.

It had dripped from the second S. She'd missed it at first, missed the warning spelled out for anyone to read and understand. It was there, above the bed, printed in large red letters, words running together in streams of paint, but still every bit as clear a message as the knife had been.

SAMSON'S BITCHES MUST DIE.

Melissa choked back a sob. All this was because of Brett. Not Rocky, but Brett Samson was the curse behind her nightmares. And this was her warning. Stay away from Brett or she would wind up as lifeless as the shapeless piece of black silk with the murderous knife buried in its bodice. Buried in the exact spot where her heart would have been.

Stay away from Brett or die. But why? What could Brett possibly know that was worth killing someone for? And why would someone think he'd share those secrets with her?

She backed away from the bed. The walls began to close in, wrapping her in their terror. She wanted to escape, to run and never stop until the nightmare had ended.

But she couldn't. Not yet. The flickering green light on the answering machine held her captive. It might contain the only clue as to who was behind this wanton destruction. She flicked the playback button.

"Melissa, this is Susie. I'm calling for your brother. He's worried sick about you. Give him a call and let him know where you are before he has every cop in the state tracking you down."

"Melissa. Marvin Brady here. I know you can take care of yourself. You've told me often enough. But I'm here for you, if you need me. And it wouldn't kill you to give me a call."

"This is Tim Jones, from the *Advocate* over in..."

The messages went on and on. Melissa stepped away, her body moving at slow speed.

"Melissa, you don't know me, but it's urgent that I talk to you. It's about Brett Samson."

Melissa spun around.

"You'll have to call me at home. I can't talk at work. It's 555-8031. Oh, and my name is Emily. Emily Sands."

Pulling a pen and small notepad from her purse, Melissa scribbled the name and number, then slipped the tape from the answering machine and dropped it and the note into her jeans pocket.

She'd listen to the rest later. Listen somewhere safer. Her brain was beginning to override the shock now, and she knew she should be anywhere but here.

She cracked the door open and listened. There were voices. No need to be alarmed. They were probably heading for the next apartment. Still, she couldn't take chances. She locked the door and scanned the room.

The knife. That was it. She'd get the knife.

The doorknob turned, and she heard the key. There was no time to run for the bedroom. She reached to the floor and picked up a broken lamp. Not much of a weapon, but better than her bare hands. She scrunched against the wall behind the door just as it creaked open.

"Son of a bi—! What the hell happened here?"

"Marvin, what are you doing here?" The lamp dropped at her feet, and she all but collapsed into the strong arms of the tall detective oblivious to the police officer standing behind him.

"Melissa, what happened? Are you all right?"

"I'm okay. At least I'm okay physically." She clung to him for just a moment, needing the comfort of strong arms around her. Then just as suddenly she pulled away, determined to stand on her own two feet. She needed a friend, but Marvin had never been willing to settle for that.

She struggled for words. "This is what happened." She waved her arm to include the whole room. "God only knows why."

"It's Rocky. That . . ."

Curses flew from his lips in a steady stream, but Melissa kept her silence. It wasn't Rocky, but she wasn't going to tell Marvin that. He'd find out soon enough on his own.

The officer turned his back on them, surveying the damage, standard police procedures undoubtedly whirling through his mind.

"We'll find out. There have to be fingerprints somewhere in this mess."

Melissa's mind whirled. "What are you doing here? Who called you?"

"Your landlady," Marvin answered, as he kicked a broken bottle out of his way.

"My landlady?" Melissa studied his expression. "Why would she call you?"

"Well, she didn't exactly call *me,* but she phoned in a report that your neighbor heard strange noises coming from your apartment, and she was sure you were out of town. Luckily, I was on duty when the call came through. I recognized the address.'' The concern he'd shown at first disappeared from his face, and his voice took on a harsher tone. ''I used to get invited over occasionally, remember?''

She remembered, but she wasn't getting into that now. She stepped away, pulling her hand from his. She'd wanted to be his friend. He'd demanded much more. She didn't have it in her. It was as simple as that. The magic had died for her three years ago, along with her innocent dreams of trust and happy-ever-after. Along with her love for Robert.

She edged farther away as thoughts of last night's encounter with Brett stirred in her mind. At least she'd thought the magic had died.

''You could have called, Melissa. You could have let someone know where you were going when you hightailed it out of town the other day.'' He moved around the room as he talked, observing the damage but touching nothing. ''Fortunately your brother's secretary rang me as soon as they heard from you,'' he continued. He walked over to her side and took her hand possessively. ''I was frantic, seeing your car like that, not knowing if you were dead or alive.''

''I'm sorry,'' she answered truthfully. Hurting Marvin had never been her intention. They'd gone through all this before. She pulled her hand away again. ''When did you find out about the car?''

''Yesterday. Texas state police gave us a call when they tracked it down as being from this area. I'm afraid I'll have to take you back to the station with me. We need a statement from you as to when it came up missing.''

Marvin walked the length of the room and then stopped, standing inches from the destroyed painting, his eyes sweeping across the total destruction. "Damn!" The word was little more than a whisper, but his hard body had stiffened into a statue of rage.

"C'mere a minute, Brady. You ain't seen nothing yet," the young officer called from the doorway of the bedroom, and Marvin immediately responded to his call. Another string of curses rolled loudly from his lips as he stepped inside.

She turned and quietly disappeared through the open door.

MELISSA GUIDED the small car through the early afternoon traffic in a daze, her thoughts whirling maddeningly through her brain. Nothing made sense.

"Samson's bitches must die." The words echoed frighteningly, accentuating the destruction that had faced her only minutes before. The words and actions of a deranged mind. Deranged or brutally calculating.

A deranged mind. A psycho. The picture Mosher had painted of Brett. But Brett was miles away in a cabin on Bayou Lachere. Besides, even if he was right here in town, what possible reason would he have for incriminating himself?

None. At least none that made sense. But there had to be answers somewhere, and she had to find them—fast. She reached into her pocket, brushing her fingers across the folded note. She swerved right, guiding the car into the exit lane and toward the nearest phone booth.

Melissa shuffled her feet nervously as a woman's recorded voice explained that she could not come to the phone at this time. Reluctantly, she placed the receiver in its cradle and climbed inside her car. Miss Sands was obviously not at home.

Too bad. The Sands woman was the one person who sounded as if she might have a few answers.

Melissa glanced at her watch. It was nearly two. She started the engine, then clicked it off. She looked at the phone number again. Six, three, five. That was an uptown prefix. It would take at least thirty minutes to get there, more if she got caught in traffic. Besides, what good would it do? If the lady wasn't answering her phone, she probably wasn't home.

She flung the car door open. Probably. Not definitely. It was common practice at her house to leave the answering machine on when she was working. It eliminated a lot of unnecessary conversations with intrusive salespeople and impersonal computers.

Melissa reached for the city phone book that surprisingly still hung from its chain. She thumbed through to Sands and down the list of Es. There was Eason, Earnest, Ely and Emmett, but no Emily. Nothing even close.

She thumbed farther. There was nothing left to do but try to match the numbers. She glanced down the page. A half column to go. Thank goodness it was Sands and not Smith or Hebert. There were pages of them.

Her finger slid down the column. That was it. The numbers matched. W. E. Sands on Napoleon Street. She copied the address hurriedly and climbed into the car.

Afternoon traffic was building to its usual frenzy by the time Melissa turned from St. Charles onto Napoleon, but neither traffic nor time seemed relevant in the stately old neighborhood. Rambling two-story houses

with wraparound porches nestled beneath giant oaks
that had stood for as long as the historic homes. Some
of the wealthiest families in the city lived here.

But not all of the homes were so well tended. Some
looked like the poor kin, wooden shutters hanging
askew, paint blistered and fading from too many torrid
New Orleans summers. Most of these had been sold and
broken up into apartments to house young profession-
als who preferred being close to the city and the myriad
of Tulane and Loyola students that moved in every fall.

A siren screamed behind her, and Melissa pulled over
to let a speeding ambulance pass. He didn't go far. The
siren faded away as soon as he rounded the curve up
ahead.

Melissa followed behind, but not for long. The street
was blocked by two police cars, their lights showering
the surrounding areas with color. She stopped across the
street from the action, pulling in behind an old Chev-
rolet occupied by two elderly women, craning their
necks to catch a glimpse of the excitement.

A uniformed policeman came out of a house and
waved away a group of neighbors who had gathered on
the lawn. "Just step back, folks. You don't want to see
what's happened in here. Believe me, you don't want to
see it."

He was right. She didn't want to see it. She didn't
have to. The picture was in the policeman's voice and
written in his face.

She closed her eyes and leaned forward, resting her
head against the steering wheel. She had already seen
more than enough for one day.

"Hey, are you all right?"

A pimpled teenage boy reached through the window
and placed his hand on her arm. Instinctively, she

jerked away. "Fine. I'm fine." Her voice was strained, she knew, but she managed a sickly smile.

"You don't look fine. You look a lot better than the woman inside that house, though. A whole lot better than her."

"I saw the ambulance. Is she hurt?" Melissa worked at steadying her voice but met with little success.

"No. Not now she isn't hurting. Won't ever hurt again. It's a hearse she'll be needing now. Not an ambulance."

"Did you see her?"

"Yeah. I saw her all right. I'm the one who called the cops. When she didn't open the door to pay for her pizza, I just pushed on it, you know, so I could yell for her. Thought the doorbell might be out of order. Miss Emily orders pizza every Thursday. That's her day off. I always try to bring hers 'cause she tips real well. She's nice. I mean, was nice."

"You just walked in and found her dead?"

"Yeah. But not right away. First I just saw the blood. She was in the bedroom, lying on the bed, but the blood was all over the house. I hope they catch the nut that did it. He deserves whatever he gets. Whatever he gets and a whole lot more."

"How...how...how did he..." The words stuck in her throat.

"How did he kill her?" the boy jumped in, eager to share the gore. "You wouldn't believe it. Not unless you saw it with your own eyes like I did. Plunged a long hunting knife right through her heart. The blood, it was everywhere, so much of it, he even wrote some kind of message with it. Wrote it all over the wall."

The nausea came in waves, and Melissa leaned her head against the steering wheel. Her body shook uncontrollably, and her heart pounded against the wall of her chest. She pushed open the car door, this time letting the nausea run its course.

the figure and her knees, rather with a
feeling that she, hungry-eyed, might keep about
to come after and her, tenas and a again. The wall of
weakness. She pulled up and she ran to be the peace as
put the makeshift his hands.?

Chapter Eight

Melissa stood in the doorway, staring at the figure on
the bed. Brett had acknowledged her return with no
more than a cursory remark about her day's absence
and then went right back to his letters. He had them
spread out on the bed, passages highlighted, words underlined in red, numbers and letters lining the pages like
a secret code.

Brett Samson, the mystery man. He'd told her about
his brother's death and his escape from the hospital, but
he'd evidently left out a few details of his plight. Small
details like why someone would be looking to kill her if
she assisted him. Gory little details like why Emily
Sands was lying dead in a pool of blood after making a
phone call on his behalf.

Hidden details she was determined to uncover.

That determination had forced her return to the
cabin. She almost hated to admit it to herself, but there
was no denying it. She was a reporter all the way to the
core. The need to know the truth, to uncover every
buried clue was in her blood as surely as the need for
food and water was in her body.

And Brett had become more than a story. When he'd
put himself in the path of exploding metal, he'd forged

an invisible bond between them. When a stranger had entered her apartment and left his death message, he'd only reinforced the weld that held them together.

Besides, she'd never been threatened into running from the truth. She wasn't about to start now.

"We have to talk, Brett."

"About what? Your destination for tomorrow's dangerous excursion? Maybe you could get your nails done or do some shopping. Then in case your mad bomber strikes again you'd be sure to look your best."

"I don't need your sarcasm. Especially not...not after what happened today." Her voice betrayed her condition, and she shivered from an inner chill.

In an instant, Brett was at her side, wrapping his arm around her, leading her to the bed.

"My God, Melissa, you look as if you've seen a ghost. What happened?" He didn't wait for an answer. "He tried something else, didn't he? That no-good, rotten, son of a—"

"It's not Rocky."

"Then what is it?" He cradled her in his arms. "What's happened to upset you like this?"

"Do you know an Emily Sands?"

"Emily Sands. Sands, let's see. There was a Miss Sands on the night shift. E. Sands, it read on her name tag, but it does seem like I may have heard one of the staff call her Emily, now that you mention it." His eyes seem to bore into hers, to search for the reason behind her questions. "How do you know her?"

"I don't. I only know she's dead."

"Dead? Emily? It must be a different Emily. The girl I'm thinking of is young, no more than twenty-five or so. Real nice, too. One of the few people at the hospital you could say that about."

"It's the same girl," she said with a certainty she couldn't explain.

"What are you talking about? What happened?"

"She was murdered. Someone put a knife through her heart." The gruesome words poured from Melissa's mouth, choking her with their vileness.

Brett rose from the bed and walked over to the window, staring into the gathering darkness, the muscles in his jaw clenched tightly. "Why? Why would someone kill Miss Sands?"

"That's what I want you to tell me."

"Wait a minute." Brett swung around to face her. "You surely don't think I had anything to do with this. My God, Melissa, you can't believe I killed Miss Sands."

"No," she answered honestly, "but somehow you're behind it. You may not mean to be, but you are."

Brett walked toward her, stopping a few feet away. Their gazes locked. "Just say what you have to say." He rubbed his hands across his forehead and then reached for the bottle of aspirin on the table. "I'm having enough trouble making sense out of things without you talking in riddles."

She watched him down three aspirins and then finish off a glass of water. Aspirin, the only drug he had access to. Was that why he gulped it down like candy?

Brett joined her on the bed. "I'll be as honest with you as I can, Melissa. I expect you to be the same with me." He took her hand in his. "Miss Sands was on duty the night I escaped. I called her into my room. She had the keys I needed to walk away. I tied her up in the sheets and gagged her. I had no other choice. But I didn't hurt her. I swear. I didn't hurt her."

"I believe you." And she did. That worried her most of all. She always believed him. But was her intuition misleading her now as it had once before? As it had the one time she'd let her heart dictate instead of her brain?

She felt the warmth of his hand on hers, smelled the musky scent of his masculine body, sensed his nearness, and she knew how easy it would be to let her barriers drop completely. After three years of frigidity, her heart and body longed to thaw at the hands of the rugged mystery man. The man with nothing but trouble to offer.

"Help me to understand. Tell me what happened the night you were admitted to the hospital."

"I'll tell you what I remember, but it's not much." He let go of her hand. "It was one week to the day after my brother's funeral. I had spent the morning in the rose garden searching for the missing diary. After a week of studying every line in his letters, I knew that Jason's death was not an accident."

Brett stood and began to pace the room. "I confronted Sylvia that afternoon with my suspicions. I told her my bags were packed. I would be out of Samson Place by morning, but I reminded her that the house was half mine. I would return to the garden whenever I chose, and she was not to try to stop me."

An icy shiver snaked up Melissa's spine. Brett's voice rose in anger even now. His movements were shaky, his tone agitated. Drug-induced paranoia, that's how Dr. Mosher had described Brett's actions the night of the attack.

"And how did Sylvia react to this revelation?" She managed to keep her tone calm.

"Strangely enough, like a loving sister-in-law with nothing to hide. Her performance was so good she almost fooled me."

"What do you mean?"

"Butter would have melted on her forked tongue. She insisted I stay on at Samson Place. Said she welcomed my investigations, if that's what it took to prove to me that she had loved my brother dearly. Told me how she was still in a state of shock at his death."

Brett shook his head as if clearing away cobwebs of forgetfulness. He talked slowly, deliberately, choosing each word. "She said I must have mistaken that shock for lack of caring. She implored me to join her for dinner that night, a new beginning to our relationship. For Jason's sake."

Brett stopped in mid stride. He took a handkerchief from his pocket and wiped his forehead. "For Jason's sake." He spit out the words contemptuously. "If that was not enough to warn me to beware, her next action should have been. She let all the servants off for the evening, a strange move indeed for a woman who never lifted a finger to help herself. So they could attend some festival in town, she explained."

Brett sat down beside Melissa. Her heart urged her to reach out to him, to ease his anguish. But her mind held steadfastly to the need to keep her distance, to keep her emotions at bay. She waited quietly, her hands resting in her lap while he continued the story.

"Sylvia chattered on and on mindlessly throughout the meal. When we finished, I tried to excuse myself. She wouldn't hear of it. She insisted we adjourn to the living room while she served an after-dinner coffee. She had something to tell me, something about my brother that I didn't know."

Brett stared off into space. "The rest is really hazy. I remember questioning her about the taste of the coffee. But she brushed off my comments, assuring me it was just because I was used to my New Orleans blend of chicory and strong black coffee that I found her flavored gourmet coffee a little sweet."

Melissa studied Brett's profile, the stubborn set of his jaw, the mouth circled with lines of past laughter rigid in bitterness.

"And I bought it. Like some innocent jerk, I drank the drugged concoction while she droned on and on," he continued, his voice low and hard. "My eyes were so heavy. I couldn't hold them open. When I finally realized what was happening, I tried to get out. But I'd waited too long."

Brett rubbed the back of his neck with his left hand, stroking the tight muscles. "It was crazy," he continued. "Like climbing off a ride at a carnival. The room began to spin, and my knees couldn't hold me up. That's when I heard her laugh, soft at first then wild and unbridled. Laughing so that I wanted to silence her forever, to choke every ounce of life from her murderous body."

His voice cracked, and Brett buried his head in his shaking hands. "It must have been like that for Jason, too. Only for him it would have been a hundred times worse. This was the woman he loved. The woman he'd vowed to spend a lifetime with. How could she just snuff his life away?"

Forgetting her resolve, Melissa inched closer. She slid her fingers down Brett's arm and then curled them around his clenched fist. Gently, she massaged away the strain, until her small hand could move inside his much larger one. The grief was tearing him apart, punishing him, refusing to let go. He longed only for revenge. Until he had it, he'd never be free.

He raised his head, an expression of stone settling on his marble lips. "The next thing I remember was waking up in a padded cell, my arms bound to my body like some dangerous lunatic. A danger to myself and others, that's what the doctor said as the orderlies poked a needle into my arm and shoved me onto a hard cot."

Contempt hardened his voice. "Score one more for the cunning murderess."

Melissa placed a comforting arm around his shoulder. Brett pulled away. He knew how to give solace, but not how to take it. He straightened his back and held his head high.

"Don't waste your sympathy on me, Melissa. It's Jason who suffered. But Sylvia isn't going to win. She'll pay. I swore on Jason's grave she'd pay, and I always keep my word. That's why I must find the diary."

The diary. That was the problem. Everything hinged on a diary that might not even exist except in Brett's mind. "Do you really think Jason knew his wife was trying to kill him and that he did nothing to stop her? Nothing but make notes in a diary that he kept hidden in the garden?"

"No. Of course not. If he'd suspected that, he'd have had her thrown off the place. He was honest and trusting, always had been. There wasn't a deceitful or mean bone in his body, but he wasn't a weakling."

"I don't get it. If he didn't suspect his wife, then why do you think the diary is so important?"

"I said he didn't suspect his wife of murder. I think he suspected her of other things."

"Such as?"

"A nasty little affair."

"What makes you think there was another man?"

"I know her type." Sarcasm shot through his words. "And I walked in one day on the tail end of a phone conversation. She tried to cover it up with a nervous laugh and a lie about her mother calling all the time, but the 'I love you' I heard was not the daughterly variety."

"Women have affairs every day, Brett. They get over them or they get a divorce. They don't murder their husbands. Why would Sylvia be any different? What reason could she possibly have to kill a man who loved her, a man who you admit would never do anything to hurt her?"

"The best reason of all. Six million dollars."

A low whistle escaped Melissa's lips. Six million. Women had killed for far less. A woman with that kind of money could buy anything she wanted, including the services of a respected doctor with expensive tastes. And she'd have plenty of clout. Enough to easily convince a judge to sign the commitment papers.

Brett reached for the pitcher of cool water that rested on the bedside table. He filled his glass to the top and once more drained it. "It's cold in here, Melissa. Freezing cold."

Melissa was usually the cold one, the first to don extra clothing and turn up the heat, but the afternoon sun had left the bedroom toasty warm. Besides, she was not ready to drop the subject they were on for talk of the temperature. "How do you know Sylvia hasn't already found the diary?"

"I don't. I only know that the diary is my best chance of proving her guilt. That's why I have to get out of here tomorrow and find some way to look for it without being detected. One false move, and I'm back in that damnable hospital, and this time they'll probably throw away the key.''

"Right. That's exactly why you can't go to Sylvia's.''

"I have no choice." His voice grew strained. "I'd like to stay up with you, Melissa, but I'm really tired. I don't understand it. I never rest in the daytime, but today it seemed like I couldn't get enough sleep. And my right arm aches like crazy. Guess I fell on it during the explosion. It's not bruised, though.''

Melissa ran her fingers across his brow. His skin burned beneath the coolness of her touch. She circled her hand to touch his bandaged shoulder. His lips tightened, and she knew he was still fighting the pain.

"Let me have a look at that shoulder, Brett.''

"No," he insisted. "It's fine. Cotile tends it. No need for you to bother.''

"It's not fine, and you know it. You're burning up with fever, and you winced with pain when I barely brushed my hand across it.''

"Don't worry. Cotile is doing everything she can. I just need rest. Rest and aspirin." He reached for the bottle again.

"Be reasonable, Brett. An aspirin overdose won't help you. And Cotile is not a doctor.''

"I'm going to bed." He wrapped his arms around his shivering body.

"Fine. You do what you think is best. I'm not your keeper. But you'll have a difficult time proving Sylvia's guilt from the grave.''

Brett collapsed onto the bed. "I'm fine," he whispered again, as he rolled onto his stomach, pulling the covers over him. "I'm just a little tired. And cold. Nights in Wyoming were never like this.''

Melissa watched and waited. Watched as the fever and chills shook him into submission. Waited until his body gave in to the fatigue and his eyes closed. Only then, when he could no longer fight her good intentions, did she ease the flannel hunting shirt from his bruised shoulder. Carefully she pulled the thick bandage away from the skin.

Her hand and body recoiled at the sickening sight that greeted her. What had once been only a tiny wound where she had removed a bit of metal was now a gaping bed of infection. Pus oozed from the reddened center of a festered circle of blistery skin.

Cotile's potions were no match for this fury. And no one would know that better than Cotile. If she had seen this today, she would have already called a doctor. There was only one explanation. Somehow Brett had kept it from her, just as he had tried to keep it from Melissa.

She replaced the bandage and pulled the covers around his fever-racked body. Time was running out.

MELISSA SAT on the top step of the porch and watched the sun rise over the marshy grassland beyond the bayou. She breathed a sigh of relief. The sleepless night had seemed an eternity. She'd stayed by Brett's bedside, bathing his burning flesh with alcohol until it had cooled to near normal.

But now the fever was rising again, and Melissa had grabbed one of her brother's sweatshirts and come outside to greet the dawn. As soon as it was light enough to see, she'd follow the bayou to Cotile's place.

She'd know who to call. They'd both known all along it might come to this, although they'd never mentioned it to Brett. He'd fight it. As sick as he was, he'd still fight seeing a doctor. But there was no choice.

Melissa walked into the house and down the narrow hallway to Brett's bedroom. He slept fitfully, sometimes writhing and moaning softly. But he slept. She wouldn't wake him to tell him she was leaving. If he looked for her, he'd see the car parked down the road, half-hidden by the trees, and he'd know she hadn't gone far.

She pulled on a pair of her brother's rubber boots. They were a few sizes too big, but they'd keep her feet dry. She grabbed a flannel shirt and pulled it over the two layers of clothing she already wore. The early morning air was nippy, but not as cold as yesterday. It would warm up as soon as the sun rose a little higher.

Louisiana weather. Bitter cold for a day or two then back into the sixties. Predictably unpredictable. Like her life.

She'd spent many a sleepless night the last few months putting together the evidence to put an end to Rocky Matherne's bloody rule. Now she was playing hide-and-seek with another killer, and as yet she had no idea why.

A fish jumped in the bayou, and a small brown rabbit hopped out from the palmettos, but Melissa had no time to enjoy the scenery. No time for enjoying anything. Her mind was far too cluttered with the problems at hand.

Somewhere there had to be some clues. Explanations as to why Emily Sands had been murdered. A reason for her own life to be threatened by someone who considered her one of Brett's women.

The memory of her bedroom clawed at her stomach, the stench of the murderous intent clogging her lungs.

She picked up her pace. She had to get there before Cotile took off on one of her fishing or hunting trips. They'd find a doctor. Then her mind would be free to concentrate on other matters. Things like who wanted her dead, and why.

Six million dollars. It was likely that figured into the equation somewhere. Six million dollars and a grieving widow. Or not grieving.

Greed could explain killing a husband. It could also explain having a suspecting brother-in-law committed to a psychiatric hospital on trumped-up charges. But how would Emily Sands's death figure in all of this? And, even more pressing, why would Melissa's name be on the death list?

There could only be one reason. Someone must be convinced that she knew a whole lot more than she did. And that someone must know she and Brett were together, or at least that they had been together.

But how could they? Unless they'd followed her. Unless they were merely playing a deadly game of cat and mouse with two people in an isolated bayou cabin.

Melissa gritted her teeth and stared defiantly ahead. Everything was only assumption at this point. And good reporters never put too much stock in assumptions. It was facts that counted.

A good reporter. She might not be great yet, but she was good. And she planned to get a whole lot better. It was more than a job. It was a calling to her. The killer hours, the disillusionment, even the danger. They were nothing compared with the thrill of breaking the big one.

Funny, when she'd first discovered her love for writing, she'd wanted to pen fiction. Romance and fantasy,

happy-ever-after. She'd taken every creative-writing and
literature course she could fit into her schedule.

She'd majored in journalism only to pacify her prac-
tical dad who was footing most of the bills. Writers
usually end up broke, he'd complained. You need a degree in something that can land you a regular pay-
check. Teaching, he'd insisted, now that's a degree for
a woman.

But she'd held out for something in the writing field,
and journalism had been their compromise. The compromise and the catalyst that had led her to heartbreak.

Robert Galliano, Louisiana's golden boy, the voice of
one crying in the wilderness, the one who'd led the state
from political corruption to heights of glory.

No matter now. It was all behind her. She'd been
taken in completely, but she'd learned a valuable lesson. Never take things at face value. And, most of all,
never trust your heart.

The sound of footsteps interrupted Melissa's bitter-
sweet reverie. She whirled just in time to see a figure
move from a clearing and disappear into a scattering of
cypress trees.

"Cotile," she called and hurried off, away from the
peaceful bayou and into the surrounding swampland.
"Cotile." Her right foot bogged down, and she clutched
at a protruding cypress tree, pulling herself to an upright position.

"Cotile," she called again, but her only answer was
the cawing of a loud crow, probably laughing at the
strange city woman trying to maneuver through the
boggy terrain.

"Face it, Melissa," she told herself, loudly enough
for the crow to hear. "You're starting to lose it. If that

had been Cotile, she would have easily heard your loud mouth. Your tired eyes are playing tricks on you."

It was just a shadow. Nothing more.

A wave of apprehension welled inside her. She'd taken every precaution, but there were no guarantees she hadn't been followed yesterday. Someone could have easily spotted her. At the doctor's office or at her apartment. Even at Emily Sands's.

Melissa forced herself to push ahead. This was no time to become paralyzed with fear. She had urgent business to take care of.

Cotile's cabin was in plain sight, and there was smoke coming from the chimney. She was not only home but up and about. Together they'd find some way to get Brett the help that would save his life.

For now, her other problems would have to wait.

"YOU SOME OF Miss Cotile's kin?"

Melissa tapped her fingers against the counter. It had been after eight o'clock before Cotile could get in touch with her nephew in New Iberia. And it had taken Melissa another thirty minutes to drive to this hole-in-the-wall drugstore. Now she was having to stand around and wait while the aging pharmacist satisfied his curiosity.

"No, I'm just a friend. Cotile cut her foot. That's what the medicine's for. I just volunteered to pick it up for her. You can't drive on a bad foot, you know."

"Stepped on a piece of metal, that's what Billy said when he called the prescription in. He's Cotile's nephew. Raised right down the road. Always was a smart one. Never thought he'd be a doctor, though. But you just never know."

"That's true." Melissa pushed her other purchases toward the register, hoping he'd take the hint and ring everything up instead of continuing his monologue.

"That other guy staying at Cotile's, that your husband?"

Apprehension darted through Melissa's veins and settled in her stomach like lead. "What guy is that?" Fortunately, she managed to steady her voice if not her nerves.

"Young fellow. 'Bout your age. Not much on talk, though. Came in yesterday looking for some kind of ammunition. Bullets for a pistol, a .38. Couldn't help him, though. I don't carry that stuff around here. Not much on guns myself. Don't even hunt."

"What did he look like?"

"Blond hair, and tall. Real tall, well over six feet. And big. Not fat, just big. And, like I said, not a bit friendly. Asked for what he wanted and then left. You say he's not your husband?"

Melissa shook her head, her mind going over every possibility.

"That's good. Good for you. I never trust a man who won't talk to strangers. If you ask me, a man like that's got something to hide."

"If he didn't talk, how did you know he was staying with Cotile?"

"Well he's not from around here. If he was, I'd know him. And he was driving Cotile's old pickup. Drove right up to the pay phone out there and made a call. Then he came in here and asked about the bullets."

The tenseness slipped away, and Melissa flashed a sincere smile. "It couldn't have been Cotile's truck. It's not running."

"Oh, it was Cotile's all right. The same truck she's had for years." He finally got down to business, totaling her purchases and slipping the aspirin and bandages into the bag as he talked. "Yeah, I'd know that truck anywhere."

Melissa only half listened to the rest of his chatter. He was telling her about the medicine, explaining something about the tetanus injection and the pills. But she couldn't concentrate on mundane things Cotile would already know, not while frightening possibilities relentlessly attacked her fragile control.

She'd returned to the cabin yesterday with her determination wrapped around her like the bandages of an ancient mummy. She didn't know how much of Brett's scenario of what had happened was true, but she was sure of one thing. He couldn't be responsible for what had happened in her apartment or at Emily Sands's apartment. He was safely hidden away at Bayou Lachere, miles from the tragedies, with no possible means of transportation.

No transportation but a battered old pickup that wouldn't even start.

Assumptions. She'd warned herself about those. She obviously hadn't heeded her own warning.

She mumbled a word of thanks as she picked up her packages and hurried toward the door. The pharmacist was still talking when she pushed into the glare of the morning sun.

Melissa never looked back as she sped down the narrow highway to the cabin. She was letting her fears magnify, becoming as paranoid as Mosher had accused Brett of being. One minute buying Brett's theory completely, the next minute imagining his hand on the cold steel handle of the deadly hunting knife.

If the truck really did run, then Brett had the opportunity. But opportunity did not equate with valid evidence. And it did not provide motive. Besides, Brett was interested in only one thing. Finding the telltale diary. If he had been able to travel at all, he'd have gone to Samson Place, not to New Orleans.

The druggist may have been mistaken. One battered old pickup looked like any other to her, and she'd seen enough of them on the road lately to know there were plenty around. The area crawled with hunters. A tall blond one in a beat-up truck that looked like Cotile's couldn't be all that rare.

And even if Brett had managed to get Cotile's truck running long enough for a quick trip to the pay phone, that was no reason for concern. In fact, her only concern had to be getting the medicine to Brett, getting it into his system while he still had a fighting chance.

The doctor and the druggist had issued warnings about the seriousness of infection. If swelling or redness developed, it was imperative that the doctor be called.

Swelling, redness, fever, chills, inflamed joints. They were all present. Present and probably growing in intensity.

Melissa increased her speed, not slowing until she turned onto the dirt road that wound down to the cabin. Speed was impossible here, but still she moved at a steady pace, carefully swerving to miss the sections where the recent rains had washed away huge portions of the road.

It was nearly nine-thirty before she was finally able to throw the gear into Park and grab the precious medication. She jumped from the car and headed down the muddy path toward the cabin. The sooner Brett started on the pills, the sooner they could all rest a little easier.

A tangled vine tugged at her leg. With a quick jerk, she pulled it loose, but the other foot slipped on the muddy soil, sending her stumbling forward. She reached out her hands to steady herself.

A strong hand reached out to catch her.

Instant panic struck her nerves like an electric shock. She tried to pull back, but the force of the fall propelled her forward, pitching her against the solid male frame that appeared from nowhere.

She struggled for release, but his arms tightened around her. Jerking her head back, she stared into the piercing blue eyes of her surprise guest. She pushed against his chest, her voice razor sharp as it cut through the humid air.

"How did you find me?"

Chapter Nine

Melissa jerked free and threw her head back haughtily, challenging Marvin Brady's intrusion into her secluded hideaway. She repeated her question. "How did you find me?"

"A lucky guess." He looked around as if seeing the area for the first time. "You always talked about this place. Your haven in the swamp."

He pulled a faded hunter's cap over his eyes to shade them from the mid-morning sun. "You said you came here when the world closed in around you." His voice softened and he reached for her hand. "I figured you had to feel like that yesterday."

"You're right." Yesterday and today, she admitted to herself. But having Marvin show up was not making it any easier. And the scariest part was she hadn't even checked for signs of an intruder when she'd jumped out of the car. She'd been intent on only one thing. Getting Brett the medicine he needed.

She scanned the area. Marvin's car was parked on the west side of the house, beyond the toolshed. Although hidden from easy view, she should have spotted it. Or at least she should have noticed a new set of tire prints on the damp ground.

She was getting careless, making foolish mistakes. She'd have to get her act together if she didn't want to show up in the daily obituaries column. This time it was Marvin. Next time she might not be so lucky.

"Why did you run out on me yesterday?" His voice took on a familiar, demanding edge.

"I wasn't up to answering questions."

"You could've told me that. I know I come across like a hard-boiled detective. But I'm not without feeling, you know." His gaze raked across her, stopping to meet her eyes. "Especially where you're concerned."

Melissa backed away. The last thing she wanted was to go through all this again. She liked Marvin just fine. As a friend. Why couldn't he accept that?

"I just needed to get away," she explained, keeping her voice calm. "To have time to think. It was quite a shock finding my apartment in shambles."

"I'm sure it was. But I told you I need you to come in for questioning. I'm trying to help you. It's my job. You were out of line to just run away like that."

And she needed to run again. Fast. Before the brilliant detective figured out that she wasn't alone.

"It's nice of you to be concerned," she offered sweetly, "but I'm doing fine. A day or two more of solitude. That's all I need."

Marvin studied her expression with an unnerving intensity. She shifted her feet restlessly, anxious for him to be on his way. She hoped he'd abide by her wishes and not bombard her with questions she had no intention of answering. At least not honestly. And she'd already been told she was a terrible liar.

"I didn't track you down to harass you, Melissa. It's your safety I'm worried about."

"And I appreciate that. Honestly, I do. But no one is going to find me out here."

"I did."

"True," she admitted grudgingly. "But then you're a first-class detective. And you haven't answered my question yet. How *did* you find this place?"

"I called your brother's office. He wasn't in, but I told his secretary you were in danger. She couldn't have been nicer. Faxed me a great little hand-drawn map your brother keeps around for his hunting buddies."

"Ah, yes. My brother does have a helpful secretary." And now that she knew Melissa's whereabouts, there was no telling who she'd be able to help. Suddenly the cabin seemed a lot less safe.

Marvin reached over and pushed a wisp of her dark hair, tucking it neatly behind her ear. "You are in danger, you know. The man who broke into your apartment yesterday means business. If you'd been there... You're a smart lady. I don't have to say any more."

No. She knew the rest all too well. She'd been lucky. Emily Sands hadn't been so fortunate. "Did you get fingerprints?"

"We got them, all right. He wore gloves, but he made one big mistake. They always do."

"What was that?" she questioned, prying for details now that she knew Marvin had facts.

"He threw the gloves and an empty paint can away in the trash bin behind your apartment. And the can had his prints all over it."

"Someone with a record?"

"A mile long. Everything from impersonating a police officer to arson."

"Sounds like one of Rocky's boys."

"Right. Just as we suspected. Calvin Boutte. Drummed off the force a few years ago when he got a little overzealous in one of his arrests. Rocky gave in to media pressure, but he kept Boutte on his private payroll. Supposedly the handyman at his house in the country."

"So he hasn't served time?"

"Nothing to speak of. Rocky takes care of his own."

"Not any more," Melissa reminded him. "The party's over."

"Thanks to you." Marvin managed a slight smile before returning to business. "And it'll be over for Boutte, too, as soon as we find him."

Melissa couldn't help but notice that Marvin had avoided any mention of the Emily Sands case, although he was bound to know about it. News of murders in uptown traveled fast. And it wouldn't take a lot of brains to know the two were tied together. Not since Mr. Boutte put his intentions in writing.

She was sure Marvin had his reasons for keeping quiet on the subject. He always seemed to have reasons for everything he did. Whatever they were, she wasn't going to bring the case up. Not yet. It would only lead to questions about how she knew about the murder.

"But something still puzzles me about all this, Melissa."

Welcome to the club, she thought, but she kept silent.

"Exactly what is your connection with this Samson character?"

Melissa swallowed and tried hard to keep a poker face. There it was. Out in the open. Marvin was fishing now. And he would have done his homework. He'd know all about Brett, probably more than she did.

He was all cop. All black-and-white without any shades of gray. Unless it fit his own needs.

White would be returning Brett to the hospital.

The package grew heavy in her hand. The medicine Brett needed so desperately would not do him a bit of good until she got rid of Marvin. And if she gave the wrong answers to his questions, it might be impossible to get rid of him. She stalled for time.

"Samson... let's see. If I remember my Sunday school lesson right, he was the strong man with long hair. The one that tangled with the wrong woman."

"Cute, Melissa. But no more games. I want to know who's been in the cabin with you, and I want the truth."

"No one." The words flew to her mouth too fast. She knew he hadn't missed her surprise. Catch the respondent off guard. A questioning technique she'd used herself on more than one occasion.

"No one but Cotile," she answered, her voice steadier now, her tone as relaxed as she could make it. "She's a neighbor from down the bayou. She's been up to visit several times. Might even be in the house right now, for all I know."

"The truth, Melissa." Determination hardened Marvin's voice.

She stole a quick glance toward the house. All was quiet. And dark. There was no way for her to know if he knew someone was in there or if he was bluffing. But she'd have to find out.

"I don't want to argue with you. I appreciate your concern, your coming all the way out here to check on me. But, as you can see, I'm fine. And I'd like for you to leave now. I'm sure you have plenty to do. Like finding and arresting our friend Boutte before he strikes again."

Melissa turned and took a step toward the cabin. Marvin grabbed her arm and pulled her back. "Nice speech, but I don't buy it."

Melissa stared at him coldly. Persistence. Never willing to take no for an answer. That had been one of his most annoying qualities the few times she had gone out with him. It still was.

His grip tightened on her wrist. "I want answers, Melissa. What do you know about Brett Samson?"

She jerked her hand free, defiantly planting it on her hip. "Nothing."

"Obviously not. Not if you're letting yourself get involved with him in some way. He's a dangerous man. A mental patient who should be hospitalized."

"And I suppose you have that on the best authority. Probably talked to the doctor himself," she quipped, her patience exhausted.

"No, not to the doctor. To the policeman who answered Sylvia Samson's call for help the night she was attacked by Samson."

"Why are you telling me all this? I told you, I don't know any Brett Samson."

"And I hope you're telling the truth. For your sake."

Melissa felt a sudden tightening in her chest. She might be able to discount Dr. Mosher's theories. But not Marvin's. Whatever he said, he believed. You could make book on it. He might be demanding and possessive, but he was honest.

But his believing it didn't necessarily make it so. A woman with six million dollars would be able to find a policeman who'd swear to any story she could dream up.

Just listen to everything, Melissa reminded herself. And keep an open mind. It was the only way to get her story. And stay alive.

But right now Brett was not a threat. He was lying inside, burning up with fever. He'd earned his injuries protecting her. She might have to turn him in eventually, if the evidence proved it necessary. But for now, she was too busy trying to save his life.

"I'll come into town and answer all your questions in a few days, Marvin. I promise. Now, if you'll excuse me, I have things to do inside." She turned and started to the cabin, her steps long and purposeful.

Footsteps sounded behind her, and Marvin caught up with her as she reached the steps. "I've been in the house." His voice was coolly challenging. "There's a man here with you, or at least there has been. My guess is it's Brett Samson."

His fierce determination convinced her that he wasn't lying. He'd been in the house, all right, and he must have seen Brett's clothing and shaving gear lying around. But evidently he hadn't seen Brett. Anxiety threatened to thaw her cool exterior. Brett was seriously ill. If he wasn't in the house, where was he?

Head high and back rigidly straight, she met Marvin's icy stare squarely. "Your guess is wrong."

"Maybe." His voice softened. "Maybe not. But I'm not leaving here without you."

"Then I take it you have a warrant for my arrest." She hated to repay Marvin's concern with cold defiance, but he was leaving her no choice. Brett needed her, and she planned to be there for him. Heaven help her, she wanted to be there.

"No warrant, but I'll get one, if that's what it takes to protect you."

"I don't know anything about a Samson, but there is someone here with me," Melissa admitted, her imagination swinging into overtime. There had to be a way to send Marvin on his way. Alone.

"But it's not what you think," she continued, lowering her gaze and softening her voice. This had to sound like a painful confession or it would never work. "This isn't easy for me to tell you."

He took her hand in his. "Don't worry. You can tell me anything."

"He's someone I've been seeing for a long time."

Marvin's fingers traced a tentative path up her arm, his grasp tightening on her forearm, but still he said nothing.

"I'm in love with him. I have been for years. I tried to forget him," she murmured, putting on the performance of her life, "but I just couldn't. That's why I had to break up with you. I couldn't leave him."

Marvin stared at her, his eyes mirroring his suspicions. "You never mentioned another man."

"No. I couldn't. I was too ashamed. He's married." She bit her lip sharply until she could manage a pained expression. "I want you to go now. I can't give up this time with him. But you don't have to worry. He'll protect me."

Bitter disillusionment painted its image on Marvin's unsmiling face. Her message was getting through.

Pangs of guilt struck her in the stomach. She had been honest with Marvin from the first, had always told him they could be no more than friends, but he had never accepted that. Now she was hitting below the belt, and it was not her style. But she couldn't back down. Time was of the essence. She had to find Brett. Had to get him started on the antibiotic.

"I'm sorry," she whispered again as she turned and slowly climbed the steps. She barely breathed until she heard Marvin's footsteps stomping down the path, away from her and the cabin.

Inside, in the cool darkness, she knew her fears were founded. She called Brett's name softly, but she was certain there'd be no response. The emptiness was as tangible as the pot of cold coffee sitting on the stove.

She walked down the hall and into the room where she had left Brett sleeping. The pitcher of water still stood on the table, and the pens of various colors lay in a pile on the floor beside the bed. But Brett's jacket was gone. And so were the letters.

The damnable letters that had Brett convinced his brother was murdered. Melissa sat on the edge of the bed. Well, she'd kept her word to Brett. Kept it even though it meant putting her life in danger and then refusing police protection.

Her debt was paid. She'd stick around another day or two, if Brett returned. She'd give him his medicine and see that he had a fighting chance to get well. After that, she had a story to trail.

And all roads were leading in one direction. To Samson Place.

The screen door slammed, and Melissa leaped to her feet, instantly alert. But it was Brett's voice that echoed through the house.

"A man you're in love with?" He stopped at the door to the bedroom, a smile easing the fevered lines in his face. "I'm glad to know you feel that way about me." He moved closer, dropping to the bed beside her.

"You heard? How could you?"

"I was awake when the car drove up. It didn't sound like yours so I hid outside until I could check it out. You didn't think I would just leave you alone with some guy that appeared from nowhere, did you?''

He pulled off his jacket and dropped it on the chair beside the bed. "I thought I was protecting you. After all, how was I to know you had your own lovestruck policeman to take care of that?"

"How much did you hear?"

"I missed the first part of the conversation. But I heard every heartbreaking word of your true confessions from my hideout beneath the steps." He slipped off his shoes and reached for the sack of drugs. "Thanks," he whispered, as he read the labels. "Cotile came over to tell me where you'd gone. She went home for something. She'll be sorry she missed the excitement."

He shook a pill from each bottle and swallowed them with a gulp of water. "But, just for the record," he added, as he lowered his head to the pillow, "*I'm* not married."

MELISSA LEANED BACK in the kitchen chair, tired but relieved. Two days on the strong drugs, and Brett was well on the way to recovery.

She yawned and rubbed her eyes. She'd spent the last hour poring over the letters. The same letters Brett had pored over for weeks. And they'd gotten to exactly the same place. Nowhere.

But she could see why Brett thought something was fishy about his brother's untimely death. Jason said he had the flu, an Asian strain that attacked the stomach and the chest. But he appeared to have survived all the symptoms. All that was left before his death was a nagging fatigue that wouldn't let go.

He'd seen his doctor several times, but the doctor had
assured him all was fine. He should be completely recovered and as good as new. His doctor had agreed with
Sylvia that maybe he needed to talk to a mental health
specialist. Depression did strange things to the body.

Jason had admitted in the letters that he did have a lot
on his mind. Personal problems that haunted him day
and night. But he'd make decisions soon, he'd written.
When he did, life would change, but it would go on.

In the meantime, he was coping, he wrote, by writing everything down in a journal. Something to keep
him focused during the long days of recovery and ac-
ceptance.

Melissa stood up and stretched, rolling her head forward to relieve muscles that were strained from spend-
ing too much time in one position. She turned and
found Brett staring at her from the kitchen doorway.

"Looks like the head nurse is wearing down." He
stepped over and placed his hands on her shoulders.
With firm strokes he massaged until the tenseness vanished, replaced by feelings far more discomforting than
mere fatigue. Feelings she didn't want to think about.

Even when he was ill, his rugged virility had continued to accost her mercilessly, slowly breaking down the
barriers she'd built up over the years since Robert Galliano. His touch was like an electric shock, moving
through each vulnerable area of her body with a force
that made her ache for more.

Reluctantly, she moved away. Emotions couldn't be
trusted. She'd relied on them once before, and she'd
been dead wrong. Brett was a story. He could not become anything more. Not if she was going to help him.
Not if she was going to help herself.

"Are you feeling better?" she asked, determined to ignore the effects his nearness had on her.

"It comes and goes. That pain medication helps, or at least it lets me sleep. The problem is I don't have time to waste on sleeping."

"You have to give yourself time to heal."

"Time's running out."

Melissa watched him pace the room in only his trousers and socks. His movements were stronger today, the muscles in his hard chest rippling below a carpet of bronze. Carelessly, he ran his fingers through sun-bleached hair that fell across his forehead in mischievous locks.

She breathed deeply. She had to clear her mind of thoughts that could only lead to trouble. "Hungry?" she asked, needing to focus on something as routine and commonplace as eating. "I made some soup. Vegetable. You need some nourishment."

"I'll try a bite. If you made it, I know it's good."

Melissa filled one of the small crockery bowls and placed it and a spoon in front of Brett. He toyed with the spoon, making circular patterns in the thick liquid.

"I read the letters, Brett, like you suggested."

He put down the spoon and waited.

"One thing is confusing, though."

"Only one thing, Melissa? You're way ahead of me, then."

She sat down in the chair next to him. "How did you get the letters into the hospital? Did Sylvia bring them to you?"

"No, but she did visit often. I refused to see her, but she came anyway, faking her sisterly concern. The letters were a slip-up, though. I'd been walking in the garden before dinner the night Sylvia had me committed.

I'd taken the letters with me, as always, searching for some word, some clue to indicate where the diary's hidden."

Brett tapped his finger nervously on the table. "When I came in, dinner was ready so I just folded the letters and slipped them into the side of my boot—the one place the cops didn't look when they frisked me."

"I think you're right about there being some type of diary," Melissa interjected. "He mentioned it several times. Writing seemed to be a catharsis for him, but..."

His smoky eyes narrowed speculatively. "But what?"

He wouldn't want to hear her next words. Ignoring her rules, she leaned across the table and took his hand in hers. She shouldn't have. A shiver of desire danced dangerously through her body. Every touch, every act, every conversation was working against her, pulling her closer to the moment of truth. The moment when passion no longer listened to logic's demands.

His hand wrapped around hers possessively. "Go on."

"Parts of the letters were rational. But not all. Some of the time his words seemed to ramble on and on without meaning. They're not the work of a..., of a sound mind." There. She'd said it.

His reaction was not what she expected. The familiar look of implacable determination highlighted his rugged features. "Jason was sound, all right. No murdering wife or conniving shrink could ever make me believe otherwise. His words are all in code. Only for some reason, I can't break it."

"Code?" Melissa eyed him warily. He was talking in circles, too.

"Yeah. I'd almost forgotten about it," Brett explained. "But Jason was always better at it than I was.

It was his idea to start with. He developed it when we were kids. One winter when he had the mumps and Mother wouldn't let me near his room."

"And you kept writing in code even after you were adults?" she questioned suspiciously.

"Of course not. That's why I think Jason had something to tell me that he didn't want Sylvia to find out. And for some reason he must have suspected she was reading the letters he was writing to me."

Melissa picked up one of the handwritten pages and scanned it until she found one of the paragraphs Brett had highlighted in yellow. "'Anderson is no match for Beauregard. Long live the valiantly brave General. He was one of us, the ill soldier whispered, not wanting his wife to overhear his secrets.' What kind of code could possibly make sense of that? Especially when the next two paragraphs are equally confusing."

Brett scooted his chair next to hers. He leaned over to study the passage, his breath feathering her face. Her concentration vanished.

Brett shuffled through the pages, laying out the other five letters. "'Look carefully above waking Beauregard's cross.'" He pointed to each word as he read it. "See, that's how the code worked. You found a paragraph that didn't fit. Then you took the first word. In the next correspondence, you would find the same paragraph, in this case, paragraph ten, and find the second word."

A cloud of disappointment settled on Brett's face. "But the sentence is supposed to make sense."

"Maybe it's not paragraph ten. Maybe it's eleven or twelve."

"No. I tried them. They make even less sense. Besides, we always used the same paragraph. All six letters had at least ten paragraphs, but only four had eleven and only two had twelve.''

He bounced the eraser end of a pencil on the oak dining table. "I'm convinced it's paragraph ten. What I don't understand is why he'd change the code. If he wanted me to solve it, why make it next to impossible?"

His hand brushed against hers as he pushed the pages away. He lingered, his fingers curling around hers with a new intensity. He scooted closer. Too close. His thigh brushed against hers, strong and sensual.

Melissa shivered, all too aware of his perilous nearness, but she didn't pull away. Brett traced a line up her arm and then trailed his fingers through her hair.

"Melissa," he murmured, his voice velvety soft, making her forget promises she'd made herself, promises that had lost their urgency. Brett had been through so much. Was still going through it, but he was reaching out to her. Reaching out for more than compassion.

He drew the back of his hand across her cheek, softly caressing with his touch and with his eyes. He cupped her chin in his rough hand and tilted it upward, his tantalizing lips waiting only inches from her own.

She braced herself, calling on every ounce of courage she possessed, and pulled away. She could deal with facts but not with romantic fantasies that would only lead to trouble.

"So, what will you do?" She forced the words, all the while fighting the dizzying current that raced through her trembling body.

"I have to go back to Samson Place."

The words dropped in the room with the finality of a bombshell.

"You can't possibly do that. One call from Sylvia and you're back in the hospital. Or jail."

"I have no choice." Brett began to straighten the letters, putting them in order by date of receipt. "I'd hoped I could reach Eric by now, but it doesn't seem to be in the cards."

"Eric?"

"Yeah, he's my partner. I tried to call him every day until I got so sick. But no luck. He's on vacation, somewhere in East Germany, meeting all the relatives he's never seen before. Even his mother can't locate him."

Melissa walked to the range and poured herself a cup of strong, black coffee. Brett was definitely beginning to open up, and she needed a clear head. Every tiny detail was important to a reporter.

"So you evidently fixed Cotile's truck and went to make phone calls? Exactly when did you fix it and where did you go to make the calls?"

"You sound like a lawyer." He scooted his chair to his side of the table. "No. Not a lawyer. A reporter. How could I forget?"

"Sorry." She'd almost blown it. She had to play this cool or Brett would close up again. If he hadn't already. "I'm just surprised, that's all. I don't think I've heard about Eric before."

Brett spooned a few mouthfuls of the soup. Slowly, the tension lines disappeared from his face. Maybe her mother had been right about the stomach being the path to a man's heart. It wasn't his heart she needed to get to right now, but maybe it would work on the tongue, as well. She had to keep him talking.

"What kind of business do you and Eric have?"

"We run an adventure business for problem kids. Or more often than not, kids with problems. We take them out into the Wyoming wilderness. Teach them to trust their own minds and bodies. And teach them to trust their companions."

Brett looked up from his soup, letting his gaze linger on her face and then travel slowly down her body. "Have you ever been to Wyoming, Melissa?"

"No." She sipped her coffee. "What's it like?"

"Like nothing you've ever seen before. Majestic. A world where nature makes the laws and mere mortals don't dare break them. A place of sights and stories you wouldn't believe."

Melissa watched his eyes change from smoke to sparkle.

"You'd love it there," he added with conviction.

"I'm sure I would. What kinds of things do you do with the kids?"

The key worked, and the door opened. Stories of Brett's adventures, everything from encounters with grizzly bears to incorrigible teenagers, flowed out like the waters of Bayou Lachere after the spring rains. There was no containing the emotions or his dedication to the kids who came to them when everything else had failed.

And with every word the bond that held them together grew stronger. Brett was determined. As stubborn as she'd thought from the very beginning. But he was more. So much more.

"One day, Melissa, when all of this is over, I'll take you to Wyoming with me."

"And what will we do there?"

A sensuous glow passed between them. It was in his smile. And in the fiery depths of his eyes. "Everything," he murmured, his glance following the lines of her face and down to the curve of her tingling breasts. "Absolutely everything."

MELISSA LAY AWAKE, only vaguely aware of the pattern of moving shadows that played across her bed in the moonlight. Her mind was busy trying to put together the jagged pieces of the puzzle that was controlling her life. She had learned so much about Brett today. About his life. His dreams.

And nothing she knew to be true about him meshed with anything she heard about him. She'd experienced his courage and his gentleness firsthand. He'd conveyed his dedication to his brother and to a world of troubled teenagers so convincingly that his feelings were almost her own.

He was a man of conviction. A man to be trusted. She'd stake her life on that.

But right now that didn't change anything. There was still a madman on the loose. And as long as there was, her life was in grave danger. Hers and who knew how many others.

She could have gone with Marvin. He'd wanted to protect her, to take her away. But she felt safe here, secluded from danger. Brett was just down the hall, only a few steps away. Recovering, but still possessing the inner strength to respond instantly to any sign of danger.

Funny the way things had developed. Just a few days ago, he had been the source of all her fears. Now he was her protector.

Besides, she still had the gun. She hadn't touched it. Not since that day when she'd hid it away in the top of her closet. The day she'd almost used it twice to destroy the wrong people.

A shadow moved across the ceiling. But something was different this time. Melissa lay deathly still and waited. Perhaps fear was playing tricks on her.

She saw it again. Her gaze followed it across the far corner of her bedroom wall. A circle of light, dim but still distinct. She eased from the bed and tiptoed to the window, the thin cotton nightshirt clinging to her hips and thighs.

She wasn't imagining things. The light seemed to float through the branches of the tall cypress trees that sheltered the cabin. A cold knot of fear settled in her stomach. She moved away from the window. She mustn't do anything to alert the intruder that he'd been spotted.

Pulling her robe around her, she hugged the wall, moving stealthily until she reached the darkened hallway. Brett's door was open. She tiptoed in, whispering, "There's someone outside with a flashlight."

The room was quiet. Completely quiet. She made her way to the bed, but somehow she knew what she'd find. The covers were pulled up, revealing the outline of two fluffy pillows. Pillows, but nothing else.

Fright welled inside Melissa, but she pushed it away. This was no time for panic. She'd seen what had happened in her apartment when an uninvited visitor came to call. And she knew what had happened to Emily Sands.

She breathed deeply, forcing air into her lungs and life into her limbs. She had to think fast. And clearly.

She peered around the room. Brett's shirt was thrown across the back of a chair, and his precious letters were still stacked neatly. Some loose pills were scattered on the top of the antique dresser. That was all. Nothing to provide a clue as to where he had disappeared to in the middle of the night.

She picked up one of the pills, rolling it in her hand as she decided what her next move should be. Whatever this was, it was much smaller than the ones the doctor had prescribed for his infected shoulder. Almost without thinking, she dropped two of them into the pocket of her robe and moved to the open door.

She listened carefully for any sound, any reason to suspect that she was not alone in the house. But only the pounding of her heart broke the potent silence.

Someone was definitely snooping around outside her window, but she may have jumped to frightening conclusions much too fast. Perhaps it was Brett checking everything out, making sure they were safe.

Or maybe he'd heard something. Or someone.

Even now he might be standing face-to-face with the madman. One thing was certain. She couldn't stand around and wait for the worst. She'd have to get the gun and check things out. She moved quickly down the hall and into her room.

She pushed the straight-backed chair over to the closet. Standing on the seat, she stretched until she could reach into the cardboard box on the shelf above the hangers. Quickly, she ran her hand through the layers of her grandmother's scarves, searching for the cold, hard metal.

She reached deeper, her movements growing frantic as layer after layer of the silken fabric slid through her fingers. She grabbed up a handful and hurled them to the floor. Then another and another.

Her nails scratched against the rough cardboard. She stood on her tiptoes, reaching into every corner of the box. This was where she had put it. There was not a chance that she was mistaken. Not about this.

Brett must have the gun. He'd had plenty of opportunity to find it when she'd gone into town. She should have known all along that he'd get it back. Should have suspected something when he never mentioned it again.

She breathed deeply, determined to settle her frazzled nerves. The missing gun was no reason for alarm. Brett had the pistol, and he'd be able to protect them.

Assumptions. There they were again. Dangerous in normal times. Deadly now.

Melissa made her way down the hall and into the kitchen. A butcher knife gleamed at her from its rack on the wall. She reached for it, but her hand recoiled in sickening recollection of the sight she'd witnessed in her New Orleans bedroom. She reached instead for the boat oar that leaned against the wall. It would do.

She pushed the back door open a crack. A bullfrog croaked in the distance, and a hoot owl screeched an eerie warning. Too bad she couldn't heed it. She eased out the screen door, cringing as its squeaking carried over the quiet swamp.

There was a movement from somewhere to the left. Footsteps and the rustling of grass. Coming toward her. She stepped into the shadows of the door.

In an instant, she felt the rush of air, heard the sound of flying metal sweep by her ear, speeding like a bullet. Her stomach lurched sickeningly. Dazed, she could only stare, memorizing every detail. The curved black handle. The long, shiny blade imbedded in the wood of the doorframe.

Her worst nightmare was real. The madman had found her. He was here, and he meant to kill her. She willed her feet to move, to carry her inside the house.

The familiar walls closed around her protectively, but she knew the safety was only an illusion. Pulses racing out of control, she moved behind the door and waited. But not for long.

Her ears alerted her first. The heavy clumping sound accosted her shaken senses. Footsteps coming steadily closer, up the creaking wooden steps and onto the porch. They paused at the door, but the moonlight gave no reprieve. It framed the figure in its light, casting the ominous shadow across the room. And now the shadow held up its hand to reveal the grisly image of its lethal weapon.

She gripped the oar and raised it above her head. She had to strike swiftly. Had to deliver a crippling blow before the madman had time to plunge the blade deep into her chest. She braced her foot against the wall.

Once more the squeak sounded its alarm. All she could see was the dark shadow. The dark shadow of a man with a knife in his hand. That was all she needed to see.

One more step. One more. Let him come. She was ready. She hoisted the oar high above her head. One more.

"Now!" she shouted, and hammered it home.

Chapter Ten

Melissa held her breath. She'd given it everything she had, but the blow wasn't solid. The man had ducked just as she swung, and the oar glanced off his broad shoulder, easing the hit to the head. But it was enough. The man groaned loudly as he crumpled and fell to the hard floor.

In one fluid movement, Melissa kicked the knife from his hand and across the linoleum floor. She lunged for the switch, flooding the room with bright light.

"Brett! Oh, no. I didn't mean… I didn't know." She fell to her knees beside him, cradling him in her arms. She'd been so sure the shadow at the door was her knife-wielding attacker. It had never crossed her mind that it might be Brett.

"Are you all right?"

He shook his head as if to clear it and then touched his hand to his temple. "Ohh… No. But I must be alive. I'd have to be breathing to feel this bad," he answered, massaging the large knot on his head that was growing into a small mountain. "What the hell is going on here, Melissa?"

"The knife. The one you were holding. Someone threw it. I thought..." She was stammering, trying to make sense out of what had happened.

Brett held his head in his hand, but his gaze moved across the room and settled on the knife. "Oh, God," he moaned. "You mean you were outside? Someone threw that thing at you?"

"That's exactly what I mean. I thought it was you. I mean, I thought you were him. I mean..." This was getting worse. She breathed deeply and slowed down. "When you walked up on the porch, I thought you were the madman who's trying to kill me."

"Too bad I wasn't. The sucker wouldn't have had a chance." A faint smile curled his lips.

"There's nothing amusing about any of this." Her emotions were on a roller coaster. Mostly downhill. "And where were you when all this happened? Out for a moonlight stroll?"

"First things first, Melissa. Let's get back to the knife story." He turned and walked across the room. Using a handkerchief to grasp the handle, he picked up the knife. He ran his fingers along the sharp edge of the blade.

"How close did it come?"

"I don't know. A few inches. Too close for comfort."

Melissa watched his face grow hard. There was not a trace of amusement. He took the knife and jammed it into a grapefruit, splattering the juice across the Formica counter. "Too damn close." He dropped into one of the chairs at the kitchen table. "Sit down, Melissa," he ordered, motioning to the chair next to his.

She studied his expression, the smoldering intensity in his deep brown eyes. She'd seen him upset, but never quite like this. She sat down and waited.

"Inches, Melissa. Twice in less than a week you've survived by inches. Your luck is running out."

A cold shiver slithered up her spine. Did he really think she needed a reminder of that?

Brett got up and strode toward the door, determination tensing his muscles to hard steel.

"You can't go out there."

He picked up the knife, ignoring her order.

"He's out there, Brett. Probably waiting for us to do something foolish like come looking for him."

"Good. Now he won't have to wait long."

Melissa watched in shock as Brett pushed through the screen door and onto the porch. "Wait," she called, her voice shaking, "I'm going with you."

He stopped and captured her with a threatening stare. "You take one step out this door, and I'll wring your stubborn little neck with my bare hands."

He stepped outside, closing the door quietly behind him. Melissa took a deep breath and gathered her quaking wits about her. Picking up the oar, she walked to the door and peered out into the dark night. She might have a stubborn little neck, but she wasn't helpless.

She squeezed her fingers around the carved wooden handle. She could pack a pretty potent blow when the need arose. She'd proved that to herself and definitely to Brett. If her hit had been squarely on target, he'd likely be out cold. She eased onto the porch.

The night was deathly quiet, as if even the creatures of the swamp had gone into hiding. Slowly, her eyes adjusted to the darkness. She moved along the side of the porch, trying to stay in the shadows. She searched for movement, listened for footsteps. There was nothing. Nothing but the tricks played by moonlight on gently swaying marsh grasses.

And a rustling noise.

She spun just in time to make out Brett's tall frame stepping from the trees, plodding toward the cabin.

"Thanks for staying inside like I asked," he quipped, taking the steps two at a time.

"Did you see anyone?" she questioned, choosing to ignore his sarcastic manner as she followed him into the cabin.

"No. But I heard him. At least I heard the drone of a car engine drifting off into the distance. So much for your theory that no one could find us here."

"But he's gone," she answered, collapsing onto a kitchen chair.

"For now. But he'll be back. Tomorrow. Or the next day. When you're not expecting him. And next time—"

"Then why did he leave now?" she insisted, her nerves not up to much more of this deadly game.

"Who knows? My guess is he likes the surprise attack. Likes to strike when no one knows he's around. When no one fights back."

Brett moved closer, his gaze boring into hers. "The other day, when I was so sick, you said some things I didn't understand."

"What kind of things?"

"You said Emily Sands had been murdered. And that I was behind it. Exactly what did you mean by that?" His voice was firm, demanding.

The day he was so sick. The day she'd been to see Dr. Mosher. The day she'd gone to her apartment.

The psychiatrist's words came back to her now in frightening clarity. Brett was a dangerous schizophrenic, a man who was convinced others were out to get him. There were no boundaries to the extremes he would go to in order to convince people that the danger was real. Not even if it meant actually endangering his life. And theirs.

But Mosher had been describing a sick individual, a man totally out of control. She'd been with Brett for days now. She'd seen him coming off drugs, seen him running for his freedom, seen him almost too sick to move. She'd heard him talk of his work with troubled youths and watched the sorrow of grief moisten his eyes when he spoke of his dead brother.

But she'd never seen one sign of the man Mosher had described.

Brett sat down beside her, reaching for her hand. "I need to hear everything, Melissa. Everything about Emily's murder. Everything about Rocky. Everything about you that might help us understand what's going on."

"I went into New Orleans that day," she answered, searching her mind for memories she'd rather forget. "I wanted to get some things from my apartment. In fact, at that point, I hadn't decided whether or not I would return to the cabin."

"But you did."

His response was matter of fact, but the message in his eyes spoke the truth. The bond between them was sparked with unspoken desire. Desire dangerously lurking just beneath the surface of every word, every touch between them.

"Yes, I came back," she answered quietly. "But not before I saw the handiwork of my attacker. He'd been to my apartment. And to Emily's."

Melissa watched Brett's expressions mirror a gamut of emotions as she told of finding her place in ruins, of seeing the knife plunged through her negligee, of reading the threat printed in crimson, dripping onto the white coverlet like blood.

"Samson's bitches must die." He spit out the words in bitter disbelief. He stood up and began to pace the room, a caged tiger with no outlet for his rage. He knotted his right hand into a fist and slammed it into the doorframe.

"What kind of sick mind could engineer such gore?" He paced again, the anger boiling inside him, his muscles flexed tautly, straining against the soft fabric of his shirt.

"What about Sylvia? You say she killed your brother. Could she be behind this?"

"Sylvia?" Brett shook his head. "No. Not Sylvia. Not directly, anyway." He ran the fingers of both hands through his thick hair. "She's a heartless gold digger. But I can't see her masterminding this. Gruesome is not her style. Tell me about Rocky."

"Gruesome is just his style. The bloodier the better. But..." The words painted on her wall still echoed in her mind. No, whoever wanted her dead thought she knew something important. And that something had to do with Brett. It was the only explanation.

"But Rocky's arrest had nothing to do with you. Or with Emily Sands," she protested.

Emily Sands. What had Mosher said? Brett had the power to draw women in, to make them want to help him, to do his bidding. "Were you and Emily friends?" Melissa questioned calmly.

"Friends? No. I wouldn't describe anyone in that hospital as a friend. But she was nicer than most. That's why I hated doing what I did to her, but I had no choice."

"Doing what you did?" Her voice quivered.

"Yeah, you know, having to tie her up and gag her. And now she's dead." Brett moved toward Melissa. He took both her hands in his and pulled her up, encircling her with his arms.

"I can't let that happen to you." He placed his hand on her cheek, stroking her smooth skin. "I can't let anything happen to you."

He cupped her chin in his rough hand and tilted it upward, his lips only inches from her own. "I've lost too much. I can't lose you, too."

Then his mouth was on hers, gentle at first, but quickly growing hard and demanding. Demanding things her body longed to give. She plunged into his kiss with reckless abandon, matching his passion, fire upon fire. She wanted to feel the pain of his brutally insistent lips, wanted her raw hunger fed with fury.

Need and desire were one now, joined in a surge of violent emotions that cried out for release. She felt his hands move to the curve of her back, circling her waist, pulling her closer. She reveled in the feel of his hard body pressing against her pliant one.

But she wanted more. Needed more. She needed all of him, the taste, the touch, skin upon skin. The need had been growing inside her for days. Maybe forever.

She ran her fingers up his chest, fumbling with the buttons of his shirt until her hands played in the thick carpet of hair that covered his strong chest. She delighted in the feel of him, in the soft moans of pleasure that tore from his mouth.

He loosened her robe, letting it swirl into a pool of white cotton at their feet. Reluctantly she let him tear his mouth from her own as he guided his lips down to the base of her neck, lingering above the swell of her breasts.

He slid his hands to the buttons of her nightshirt, his sensual movements tracing a delicious path as he loosed each one.

His hands caressed her naked breasts, his thumbs moving against her hardened nipples, arousing them to perfect peaks. His lips encircled one, sucking, nibbling, tempting, before moving to the other, letting it share in the erotic feast.

The ache in Melissa grew stronger, her body vibrating with its own flaming need. She pressed against him, the molten liquid flowing from her core, as his hands seared a path lower and lower, toward the very essence of her desire.

Hungrily, she slipped her fingers inside the rough denim of his jeans, struggling with the straining zipper.

"Melissa." His voice was husky with desire, his need overpowering. "I want you. God, how I want you." He pulled away. "If we don't stop now, I'll never be able to."

She moved her mouth to his, smothering his words with the only answer she would ever be able to give him.

Brett slipped his arms around her and lifted her, cradling her like a baby in his powerful arms. He carried her toward her bedroom and laid her atop the white sheets.

With jerky movements, he tore the jeans from his body. Melissa held her breath, exhilarated at the sight.

His naked frame glowed in the moonlight, the reincarnation of a Greek god. Her body pulsed with a need so intense she ached for his touch, for his kiss, for the feel of his passion.

He crawled into bed beside her, the fire from his longing burning into her soft flesh. Once more he sought her lips, probing and promising, propelling her into a spiral of desire.

His fingers slipped beneath the satiny softness of her nightshirt, slipping it from her shoulders. "I want nothing between us," he whispered hoarsely. His hands moved down her trembling body, his fingers burning a sensual trail past her waist, across her hips, massaging her thighs with circular movements that went closer and closer to her fiery core.

She explored his body with her hands, seeking out the places that made him writhe, made him moan in ecstasy. Her fingers moved deftly, guiding him to her. Pulling him into the passion that flowed like molten gold.

She curved her hips upward, her body begging to receive him. It had to be like this. Nothing about their relationship had been slow and calming. It had been fevered and forceful. Her craving could be no different.

"Melissa. Sweet, beautiful Melissa." Her name tore from his mouth in a moan. "I want you so much."

And he was inside her then, a pushing, pulsating rhythm of love, pulling her with him, higher and higher. Her fingers dug into his flesh, her whole being vibrating with unbridled desire. Vibrating, pulsating, her heart racing out of control.

She gasped for breath, crying out in joyous passion as they exploded together, a symphony of ecstasy. A glorious ecstasy, binding two as one.

"I love you," she whispered, as Brett's body relaxed against her. And she knew it was the truth.

Content and totally happy, Melissa lay quietly for long minutes. Or was it hours? Lay with her eyes wide open listening to the peaceful sounds of Brett's breathing. She didn't want to sleep, didn't want to close her eyes.

Moonlight poured through the window, bathing their glistening bodies. Passion spent, but still clinging as if nothing could ever tear them apart.

She wanted this night to last forever. Wanted to memorize each curve of Brett's muscular body as it entwined with hers, each line in his rugged face. Remember him just as he was now. With the feel of love still softening the hard masculinity that had become his trademark.

Memories. One week in November with a man who entered her life by chance and sparked feelings of desires that she never knew existed.

Memories of a man she'd never known before and would likely never know again. But could memories ever be enough?

MORNING CAME TOO QUICKLY.

And with it came the realization that things could not go on as they had. Life was too precious. And Melissa's stalker was too intent on seeing her dead.

She pulled the heavy flannel shirt tighter as she stood next to the pay phone, shivering while the telephone in Marvin Brady's office completed its fourth ring. "Be there, please be there," she pleaded into the mouthpiece. Now that she'd made the decision, she wanted it over with as quickly as possible.

Besides, standing at the side of the road was not the safest predicament to be in. Especially not after last night's knife-hurling incident.

But madman or not, it had been hard to leave the cabin this morning. Hard to leave Brett. The satisfied ache of her body was a poignant reminder of the passion they'd shared last night. The passion she longed to share again and again.

She'd thought she'd never learn to trust another man. Not after Robert. And the truth was, under ordinary circumstances, she might not have been able to. But these were not ordinary circumstances.

Standing in the path of death did strange things to one's psyche. In her case, it had let her learn to live.

"Marvin Brady here, can you hold on a minute?"

The strong male voice abruptly halted her reverie. "No," she answered impatiently. "I really can't."

"Melissa? Is that you? Are you all right?"

"Yes, and I need to talk to you. *Now.*"

"Where are you? I just dispatched a couple of state troopers to your cabin to check on you."

"You did what?" Surely she'd heard him wrong.

"I sent some troopers to check on you. We found Boutte."

"When? Where?"

"A couple of hours ago. But I just got word of it. The authorities over there picked him up. Not ten miles from your place on the bayou."

Relief flooded her body in waves. "How did they find him?"

"Pure accident. Can you believe it? The stupid jerk was driving around with a burned-out headlight."

"I'm not following you."

"They stopped him for a missing headlight. The officer did a routine check. Turned out they had our prime suspect."

"Are you sure it's the right man?"

"Oh, it's him, all right. They searched his trunk. Found a deer rifle and a hunting knife. Real similar to the knife he left in your bedroom."

And in Emily Sands's heart. Melissa grew weak. It was over. The constant fear she'd lived with for days could go away. But all she felt at this moment was a cold numbness. And sorrow for all the people who had loved Emily Sands.

"Do they have any idea why he targeted us?"

"No. But he's one of Rocky's boys, so you can bet the big guy orchestrated the show. We don't know the whole story yet. But we will soon. I can promise you that."

"So you think Rocky's behind this?"

"Looks that way. Our boy Boutte's not talking, but he'll sing before it's all over."

"Then what's your explanation for the Samson thing he wrote on my wall, Marvin? What does Samson have to do with Rocky?"

"We're not sure. Maybe nothing. Maybe the guy read about the escape in the paper and decided to use it to confuse the investigators, to keep the heat off him."

Maybe, Melissa mentally agreed, but probably not. Unless she missed her guess, that little story never made the paper. According to the report Marion Olson had given her, the hospital wanted it all kept quiet.

"You're safe now, Melissa. That's the main thing. But we need you to come in for questioning. The sooner the better."

"You've got it. I'll be in tomorrow. Or the next day for sure. Just report that I'm out of town for some much-needed rest. I'll be in touch as soon as I get back."

"Rest? A nice turn of phrase for what you're doing."

His sarcasm was clear even through the phone wires. She was sorry she'd had to make up the story she'd told him. But there had been no other way to get rid of him. She was surprised even that had worked. And she still needed him and his troopers to stay away.

"Oh, by the way," she added, as nonchalantly as she could manage, "call off the troopers. I don't want them anywhere near my cabin."

"Of course. We wouldn't want them to spoil your little party."

"And, Marvin, thanks for everything. You've been great through all this. I really mean that."

"Yeah, sure. You take care, Melissa. Everything's under control. At least on this end."

The phone clicked in her ear. She hated to see him upset over her affair story, especially after all he'd done to help catch the Boutte guy. But he was blowing things out of proportion. They had never really dated. She'd had dinner with him a few times. That was all, although he'd pushed her for a lot more. He had a lot to learn about women.

She returned the phone to its cradle and slid behind the wheel of her car. She'd left the cabin this morning fully intending to go to New Orleans. She had planned to go to Marvin Brady and request police protection. He was handling the case, and he knew the danger she was in.

She and Brett had talked at length, and for once they agreed. It was the only reasonable solution. But she hadn't agreed with Brett's insistence that he stay in the cabin alone. He wasn't afraid, he argued, and, besides, there was nothing he'd like better than the chance to meet the knifer one-on-one.

He planned to stay put until he could reach his partner, Eric. Or until he could think of some other way to come up with the incriminating diary.

The diary. If it actually existed, it was buried somewhere at Samson Place. So there was only one sensible thing for Melissa to do.

She pulled out onto the highway, heading north toward Baton Rouge. She kept the speedometer on sixty-five all the way, stopping only once in Lafayette to pick up a needed prop. A rented camera with multiple lenses.

Three hours later she pulled into a curving driveway that stretched for a quarter of a mile beneath an arch of ancient oaks. But even that did not prepare her for the magnificence of the home.

Samson Place, its massive white pillars pointing to the blue sky, stood at the end of the driveway, a fitting monument to the past and the glories of the old south.

Melissa took in the splendor while her mind feverishly rehearsed the story she'd concocted on the drive. She pulled up to the front gate and parked, half expecting a bevy of slaves to meet her at the walk. When none did, she made her way up the steps and lifted the pewter knocker.

A uniformed butler opened the heavy wooden door.

"I'm Jessica Green, with *Southern Homes and Gardens*," she announced in her best Southern drawl. "If you'll just tell Mrs. Samson I'm here. She's expecting me."

The butler eyed her curiously but didn't question her. Instead he asked her to step into the parlor while he informed the mistress of the house that she had a guest.

Melissa waited nervously, her gaze circling the small sitting room where she'd been placed. The Victorian chairs were covered in a soft mauve velvet, a perfect accompaniment to the rich cherry of the decorative tables. Vases of artistically arranged fresh flowers filled the air with a fragrance of springtime despite the northerly winds that howled with a vengeance around the corners of the old plantation house.

Even the rug beneath her feet whispered taste. And money. Brett had said Sylvia was a gold digger. Well, from the looks of things around Samson Place, she'd struck the mother lode.

Melissa looked up as the clicking of heels on the marble floor announced the arrival of her hostess.

"Miss Green, I'm Sylvia Samson. Washington tells me we have an appointment, but I'm afraid there's been some mistake. I have no mention of you in my appointment book."

"Oh, my goodness," Melissa crooned sweetly, "I hope I didn't put down the wrong date. I've been looking forward to this ever since we talked back in August. We're planning to make this our feature story in the special anniversary issue."

Melissa waited, studying the petite blonde with the eye of a reporter. Sylvia was not at all what she'd expected. Her hair was piled loosely atop her head with a few tendrils falling to frame her heart-shaped face. Her skin was porcelain clear, a pale backdrop for the bright red lipstick that colored her thin lips and the obviously false eyelashes that highlighted her green eyes. The exaggerated makeup on her youthful face gave the illusion of a young child playing grown-up in her mother's clothes and makeup.

"I don't remember talking with you," Sylvia answered thoughtfully. "But so much has happened since August. I lost my husband, you know."

"No, I didn't know. I'm sorry to hear that," Melissa answered, scrutinizing Sylvia's every move. If the woman was faking, she was doing an excellent job. Even her eyes were in on the act, becoming moist on cue.

"The gardens are lovely, though. My late husband always saw to it that even in the winter they were filled with life and color."

"Then I'm sure he'd want the world to share in their beauty. That's what this article would be. A tribute to your late husband and his love of nature." Melissa hated to do this, use a dead man's memory to get onto the grounds of Samson Place, but there were times when necessity had to overrule sentiment.

Oh, God, listen to her. She was beginning to sound like one of those hard-baked reporters she despised. The ones who stuck cameras in the faces of people just after their houses disappeared in a hurricane. Give the people what they want. Misery and suffering. Other people's suffering.

But she didn't want the camera on Sylvia. She wanted it on the gardens. And she wasn't even writing a story. She set a winning smile on her face and waited for Sylvia's answer.

"What exactly would the article involve? Would you have to be here long?"

"Absolutely not. A day or two at the most. I'll come in the mornings and spend a few hours roaming the gardens and taking pictures. I'd like to talk to the gardener, of course, get some tips on how he manages to keep the place in such great shape. That's it. I won't have to bother you at all. And, of course, you'll have the final say on what we print.''

It was working. She could see the signs of acquiescence settling on Sylvia's face. A feature story in *Southern Homes and Gardens* was too much for a society-loving Southern belle to refuse.

''And you're the only one who would be here?''

''Guaranteed. I work alone. It gives us better coverage in the long run. A better feel for the solitude and beauty of the gardens just as you experience them here at Samson Place.''

''And you won't print anything without my approval?''

''Not a picture or a word.''

''Well, I don't see what it could hurt, then. And it would be nice recognition, for Jason, I mean. A tribute to all his hard work. Everybody reads your magazine.''

The idea was obviously growing on her as she talked. Her eyes shone, and excitement gave her voice a bubbly quality. ''When do you want to start?''

''Now would be perfect,'' Melissa answered eagerly.

They spent the next two hours together, walking through acres of gardens. Some were almost wild, greenery and vines of every description growing at will over and around stone walkways and in and over chalky statues. Others were meticulously landscaped, every plant allotted a specific piece of earth. And fountains and sculptures, benches and wrought-iron chairs appeared at every turn, welcoming and enticing a visitor to stay and soak in nature's handiwork.

For once, Melissa was in total awe. The serenity and beauty of the gardens really were like something straight out of *Southern Homes and Gardens*. She carried her camera with her but refrained from snapping any pictures, explaining she wanted to see the whole place before she chose the specific areas she'd concentrate on for the article.

Sylvia didn't appear to suspect anything, but she might, if she saw Melissa fumble with the rented camera. Besides, if Brett's summations were on target, it was the rose garden that held the information she was looking for.

"I think you've seen everything. I'll leave you on your own now, but I do need to warn you about Ealey."

"Ealey?" Melissa questioned cautiously.

"Short for E. Lee. He's our German shepherd. Actually he was more Jason's than mine, though he's quite a protector where I'm concerned. He's usually friendly, but since Jason's death, he's been moody, especially around strangers. Ordinarily we allow him the run of the grounds, but I'll tell the gardener to keep him locked up while you're here."

"I'd like to meet him," Melissa answered honestly. "I love dogs. I'm sure we could become great friends."

"Maybe, but I'll have him penned while you're here anyway. Just as a precaution. If you truly want to meet him, just let Zeke know. He's the gardener I introduced you to earlier. Ealey's kind of adopted Zeke as master now that Jason's gone."

Melissa thanked Sylvia again, eager to be on her own. She had yet to see the famed rose garden, and it was obviously not on Sylvia's tour agenda. That was okay. She'd find the place for herself. That way she could stay as long as she wanted and snoop to her heart's content.

She left the planned paths, wandering through a clump of tall pines, heading toward the house. Sylvia had shown her everything to the east of the house but nothing to the west. So chances were the rose garden was in that direction.

Progress was slow. The area had probably been cleared in the past, but much of it was overgrown with weeds and shaggy bushes. Melissa pulled her foot loose from a tangled vine only to put it down in another. But the house was growing closer. If the rose garden was in this direction, she should see some sign of it soon.

She heard it before she saw it. The music of water cascading over and through rocks, the gurgling, frolicking sounds of a brook at play. Melissa pushed through some overgrown photinia bushes.

Her diligence was rewarded. It was all here, just as Jason had described it in his letters. The peaceful haven where he had spent his last days. Spent them writing coded letters to his brother. Letters that a wife whose love had grown cold would not be able to decipher.

Melissa set her backpack on a decorative bench and unloaded her camera. She walked slowly around each bush taking pictures of every statue, every fountain.

Finally, she sat in a wrought-iron glider. A colorful rose bloomed at her elbow, claiming its last bid for glory before the first hard freeze of winter robbed it of life. Its fragrance filled the air around her.

The garden was truly a place of beauty. So sad that for Jason it had become a prelude to death.

"Look carefully above waking Beauregard's cross." She whispered the words over and over, but still nothing made sense. There was no statue of General Beauregard here. In fact, no statues of any generals. And there was no cross.

There was nothing. No hint as to where the diary might be buried. And there was no way she could dig up the whole garden. She retraced her footsteps, choosing to fight the woods rather than have Sylvia realize she had been in the rose garden.

Besides, she wanted to stop and talk to the gardener. Zeke had been friendly enough when they'd been introduced. He might be just the source of information she needed. And it would definitely be to her advantage to make friends with the moody German shepherd that guarded the secrets of the lovely heiress and the mystery diary.

MELISSA SAT at the library desk, scanning through microfiche issues of the *Times Picayune*. She wasn't sure what she was looking for, but she had time to kill. And she'd learned early in her reporting career that the past was always a good predictor of the present.

She'd dropped off the film to be developed at a quick processing shop. She'd also made one more stop, to a drugstore in the same block. She hadn't been snooping last night when she'd found the pills in Brett's room. But now that she had them, she might as well know what they were.

Haldol. It was in common use for combating serious depression. A prescription drug, the druggist had emphasized, but one that was finding its way onto the streets.

But why did Brett have these? And why so many? It certainly didn't fit in with any of his stories. Drugs. Depression. It just didn't make sense.

Melissa stopped to read an article from the society page. Dr. Stuart Mosher escorted Mrs. Carl Hawthorne to the annual medical association's extravaganza. Melissa knew Mrs. Hawthorne. She was the young and vivacious widow of Congressman Hawthorne. Mosher had good taste, though she couldn't say the same for Mrs. Hawthorne. She scanned on.

Dr. Stuart Mosher and Mrs. Wilkerson Grafton III acted as host and hostess for the debutante party of her daughter, Monica Grafton. No doubt about it, Melissa acknowledged, the man had a weakness for beautiful women. Beautiful and wealthy.

Melissa felt the adrenaline surge through her body with potent force. That was it. It fit right in, strengthening her hunch.

Sylvia had found the doctor's weakness and was using it to her advantage. Of course, the doctor would believe her and bend over backward to accommodate.

Sylvia Samson, the beautiful, millionaire widow. She might look innocent enough, but that didn't mean she wasn't as coy and cunning as any other gold digger. Brett had probably called her right all along.

Melissa drummed her fingers restlessly, eager to get back to the cabin. She'd never meant to be this late, but getting away from Zeke had been a challenge. Worse, the lengthy conversation hadn't gained her anything except detailed facts about growing hybrid roses.

She turned her attention to the *Times Picayune,* and scanned back twelve years.

She glanced at her watch. The hour was about up. She could pick up her pictures and head to the cabin. She couldn't wait to see Brett again. She had a lot to tell him. And a few questions, too.

She started to remove the microfilm, but a small headline caught her eye.

BRETT SAMSON ACCUSED IN DEATH OF HIGH SCHOOL SWEETHEART.

Chapter Eleven

Melissa jerked her chair closer, mesmerized by the incriminating words.

Brett Samson, member of a prominent Louisiana family, arrested in connection with the murder of Ellen Lane.

The familiar quaking began. The feeling of impending doom that had come to be so much a part of her life during the past few days. It was as if there were two Brett Samsons. The one she knew so intimately, and the one that everyone else knew.

She pushed the feeling aside. Reporters had to deal with facts, not feelings. She read. It had been a car crash, and Brett had been driving. Investigating officers said he reeked with the odor of alcohol, and evidence from witnesses at the scene testified he'd swerved recklessly before the car had left the road and crashed into a tree.

He'd gotten off with only a few scratches. His girlfriend, Ellen, had been dead on arrival. Dead and pregnant.

Melissa switched to a local paper. The facts were about the same, but the coverage was much more extensive. Ellen's mother claimed Brett had forced her daughter to go with him that night to the edge of town, to a hangout frequented by a delinquent college crowd.

She had heard her daughter arguing with him on the phone earlier that evening, and her daughter had left the house in tears. Left the house never to return.

Melissa scanned papers for the next several weeks. The case grabbed daily headlines. Mrs. Lane was not about to let it die. She organized marches and protests all over the city. She demanded justice. And the justice she demanded was the charge of manslaughter. If Brett got off, she claimed, it was just another case of the rich buying their way to freedom.

She lost her crusade. The grand jury dismissed the case for lack of evidence.

Melissa moved in a daze, gathering her things and walking into the late afternoon sun. There was so much she didn't know about Brett. Their relationship had been intense, but frighteningly brief. Yet something about him always made her believe him, even when the preponderance of evidence was so squarely stacked against him.

What happened twelve years ago was not the issue. She knew that. Brett had been only a teenager then. But his character was an issue. And so was the matter of trust.

Last night, she'd made love to him in a frenzy of passion she'd never known before. It had been inevitable. Every moment they'd shared for the last few days had been sparked with fierce emotion. Every decision, every move, had been one of life and death. And with every day, the sensual attraction between them had grown stronger until the very air had crackled with it.

But when she was away from Brett, things took on a different perspective. That's when memories came back to haunt her. Memories of Robert Galliano and how she'd naively believed every word, how she'd fallen hopelessly in love with the man she wanted to believe he was.

Was she making that mistake with Brett? Mosher had said he had a way of making you fall under his spell. Pulling you in, making you eager to do his bidding. Making you want to help him.

Making you fall in love.

Now it was up to Melissa to ferret out the truth. And that meant keeping her emotions under control. She couldn't repeat last night's moment of heavenly abandonment. No matter how badly she wanted to. She would have to maintain the wall of isolation that had served her so well over the past three years. There was no other way.

She picked up the developed prints and drove to the cabin, a thousand discomforting thoughts parading endlessly through her mind.

"I TOLD YOU to stay away from Samson Place." Brett's angry voice cut like a knife.

"And I told you, I make my own decisions." Melissa lifted her chin and met his icy stare with one of her own. She had expected anger when she told him where she'd spent her day. He definitely didn't disappoint her.

"The woman is a murderer. Do you think she's going to let you just waltz in there and dig up the information that will convict her?"

"No, but she doesn't suspect a thing. I'm a reporter, remember? I know how it's done."

"Of course. You're a reporter. How could I forget? That gives you the right to interfere anywhere you choose."

"No, but it gives me the right to do my job. I don't know what your problem with reporters is, but I've told you before, I'm proud of what I do."

"I'm sure you are," he retorted, grabbing the photos and stomping out of the kitchen and down the hall.

Melissa unclenched her fists and poured herself a cup of black coffee. Brett's relief that her attacker was in jail had been quickly overshadowed by his anger. He was taking his self-proclaimed role as protector a little too seriously.

He should be thanking her for the snapshots. She'd covered every square foot of the rose garden. If the letters really contained clues as to the location of the diary, he should be able to find the spot in the pictures.

Besides, it wasn't like she'd been in any immediate danger. Even if Sylvia had killed Jason, she was far too smart to pull out a gun and shoot a visiting reporter in front of all the servants. And after today's meeting with her, Melissa wasn't at all convinced that Sylvia could murder anyone.

The heavy fragrance of garlic and andouille sausage hung in the air. Melissa lifted the lid on the big pot of jambalaya that sat on the back burner. Apparently Cotile's infatuation with Brett was still intact.

She stirred the rich rice and meat concoction, but her stomach was far too uneasy for the Cajun food. She poured a glass of milk and smeared some peanut butter on a slice of wheat bread.

Brett had the snapshots, but he'd left the letters on the table. She flipped through the pages. Beauregard's cross. Highlighted in yellow and underlined in red. Well, so much for his farfetched code theory. She'd covered the rose garden with a fine-tooth comb. There was nothing there to do with any Beauregard or a cross.

Lost in her thoughts, Melissa didn't hear Brett's approaching footsteps. She looked up to find him lounging in the doorway, his gaze direct and extremely discomforting, his mouth twisted in exasperation.

He walked to the counter and leaned against it. She turned and watched him pour a mug full of hot coffee. He was at home in the cabin. And it fit him well. Masculine and rugged, like the very essence of him.

It was one more area of her life he'd invaded. The cabin that had always been her refuge would now be filled with Brett. With the memory of him, the scent of him. With the feel of his body exploding in hers.

Warmth flooded her senses. She took a deep breath and watched him with studied awareness. So much had changed since that first night. It was hard to believe he was the same shaken, confused man who had pushed the gun in her ribs and commanded her to drive.

The glassy look had disappeared from his eyes, replaced with a piercing depth that took in everything at once. The shaking had disappeared, too, and most of the paleness. Now it was raw strength that dominated his manly features.

He even dressed the part. The jeans she'd bought him hugged his hips snugly, and one of her brother's T-shirts stretched over his strong chest. A hunting jacket, hooked by his thumb, dangled from his right hip.

Tension permeated the air in almost suffocating force. There was everything between them. There was nothing between them.

Brett drained the cup before breaking the heavy silence. "I'm going out for a while. I'll need your car." He picked up her keys from the counter and dropped them into his pocket. "I'll be back before morning."

She wanted to protest, to tell him it was ridiculous to
leave, to go looking for trouble. But she couldn't. She'd
told him she would do as she pleased. She had to accept the same from him.

"Where are you going?" she asked, keeping her voice
cool and distant.

"To take care of some unfinished business."

"Can't it wait until morning?"

"No." His stare was coldly accusing. "Not now." He
took the flashlight and pushed through the door.

She watched him as he strode quickly down the walk
and ducked into the dilapidated toolshed. Minutes later
he reappeared, his hands full, the glint of moonlight on
metal glaring ominously through the darkness. He
opened the trunk of the car and threw in a large shovel
and a rake before heading to the shed.

It couldn't wait, he'd insisted. Not now.

Suddenly his destination was clear. He was going to
Samson Place, and she was the reason. He'd been
waiting for word from his partner, for the chance to go
to the grounds legally without the threat of being returned to the hospital. Her visit to Samson Place had
changed all that.

He was afraid for her. Afraid to let her get involved
with a woman he was convinced would stop at nothing
to get what she wanted. He was risking everything. And
it was all because of her.

Melissa grabbed her coat and took the steps two at a
time. She reached the car just as Brett returned and
tossed some old rags and a wire cutter into the trunk.
He slammed it shut and rounded the back of the car,
swinging himself behind the wheel.

He stopped short, the frown on his face telegraphing
his mood. "Get back in the—"

"Save your breath. I'm going with you," she cut in defiantly.

He glared at her coldly. "Suit yourself," he retorted. "You always do."

She'd won another round, but the victory was no more than a ball of regret, settling in her stomach like a deadweight. The lines had been drawn between them. She had been his appreciated accomplice before. Now she was the interfering reporter. The one who was forcing him to make his move before the time was right. It would be a long night.

It was almost three hours later before Brett broke his silence. "Why did you do it, Melissa? Why did you go to Samson Place when I had warned you to stay away?"

"I'm not sure," she answered honestly. In fact, she wasn't sure why she'd done any of the things she'd done in the past few days.

"What is it with this death wish mentality that makes you determined to live your life one step away from the edge?"

"Don't be absurd. Did I ask to be kidnapped? Do you think I wanted some nut to blow up my car or to throw a knife at my heart?"

"The kidnapping? No. I take all the blame for that. The rest of the stuff? Yeah. I think you like being in the heat. Why else would you be an investigative reporter? You can't like playing in people's dirty linens."

"I don't play in them. I launder them so the rest of you don't have to get your lily-white hands dirty." If this was the way the conversation was going to go, she'd just as soon he continue his punishing silence. But she wouldn't back down. "I don't look for trouble. I just don't run away from it. There's a difference."

"Going to Sylvia's was looking for trouble." His voice had grown softer, exposing the concern that was driving him tonight. He placed his hand on the back of the car seat and stretched it out until his fingers wound through her hair. "Just getting involved with me is probably trouble enough," he added quietly. "It always has been."

He was obviously right on that score. It definitely had been trouble enough for a young girl twelve years ago. And it had been enough for Emily Sands. But somehow that had to do with Rocky, not with Brett. Getting involved with Brett would only mean danger for Melissa if she let down the barriers that protected her heart.

Brett turned off the highway at the same exit Melissa had followed to Samson Place earlier that day. He slowed a little on the curving road. It was only eleven, but the highway was all but deserted. He rounded a corner and then swerved onto an unmarked dirt road.

"Where does this go?"

"To the south side of the gardens. Along the old creek that borders the place. We shouldn't run into anybody back here. No one at all."

The front wheel dipped into a pothole, jerking the whole car. "Road's even worse now than it was back when Jason and I used to hunt around here."

The touch of sadness in his voice that always accompanied Jason's name tugged at Melissa's heart. She wanted to keep him talking, but not about his dead brother. "When did you move away from Samson Place, Brett?"

"Twelve years ago. The year I graduated from high school. I was supposed to leave that fall for college."

"But you didn't?"

"No. Things didn't work out."

His voice seemed distant, almost hollow. It was best not to probe further. She couldn't chance his retreating into one of his silent, brooding moods. Besides, she'd had a crash course this afternoon on his life twelve years ago.

Once more he laid his arm on the back of the seat. Slowing down to avoid more rough spots in the road, he inched his hand closer, tracing his thumb along the lines of her neck to the tip of her earlobe and down again.

He stared straight ahead, lost in a world of memories. Even so, he reached out to her with a touch as soothing as summer rain.

"I lost someone that summer," he continued, his voice low, almost as if he were talking to himself. "Someone who meant the world to me."

Brett turned again, this time heading due north and straight toward the house. The roofline of Samson Place came into view, rising above the treetops like an ancient castle.

"It must have been difficult for you, leaving a place as beautiful as this."

"Not then. I had to leave. I couldn't live with the memories. I signed my rights to the business away, keeping only a half interest in Samson Place and a hundred thousand dollars cash for myself. With that, I thought I was getting more than I deserved."

A hundred thousand dollars. A tidy little sum to her, Melissa acknowledged, but not to a boy with a multi-million-dollar inheritance waiting in the wings. The rich buy their way out of trouble. That was the cry of Ellen Lane's mother. If that's what Brett had done, he'd obviously assessed himself a larger cost than the courts had.

"I bought a fast car and took off, down every highway and back road until the memories began to fade away into a dusty blur. Then, when my money was running out, I ran into Eric. He turned my life around. The guy had a dream. That was a whole new concept for me, so I joined up with him. I threw in the few thousand I had left, and together we began the Wilderness Youth Experience."

"And Eric can get you formally released from the hospital," Melissa pleaded. "That's all it would take. A flesh-and-blood witness with some legal documents."

"What you mean is someone to contradict all those lies my loving sister-in-law spread about my being a dangerous nut, don't you?" Contempt for Sylvia gnawed away at his composure, edging his words with disgust.

"Please wait for Eric, Brett. You're bound to hear from him soon."

"I've waited too long already."

Brett's body grew rigid, and Melissa took his hand in hers, massaging the strained muscles. Her heart ached for him. For a young boy who'd lost too much. For a man who'd lost again.

Brett steered off the road and close to a barbed wire fence. He stopped the car and shifted into Park. Melissa started to scoot toward the passenger door, but his strong grasp on her hand stopped her.

He wrapped his arm around her shoulder and pulled her closer. His hand cupped her chin, tilting her face toward his. His lips were close, so close. And then they were on hers, probing, demanding.

She struggled for breath, pulling away from his all-consuming need, desperately fighting needs of her own.

He loosened his hold, capturing her gaze and holding it with his smoldering stare. "Okay, lady, you wanted to come on the hunt. Now it's time to face the grizzly."

He pushed away from her and opened his door, swinging his long legs around. He climbed from behind the wheel in one easy motion, then rounded the car and opened the trunk.

Melissa watched as he took out the tools, laying them next to the fence. She went to join him. "I'll take these," she offered, picking up the shovel and the wire cutters. She had demanded he let her come with him. She'd pull her weight.

Brett pushed the equipment through the barbed wire. Then, using his foot and one hand, he pulled the wire apart for her to climb through the fence.

"This is trespassing, you know. People get shot for this."

"It's not trespassing for me. I own half the place."

True. She jumped as a shadow played eerily over the path. They might not be committing a crime, but somehow the fear of getting shot was not alleviated.

"Exactly where are we?" she asked after a half-mile trek through vines and mud and various sticker bushes.

"Exactly, I couldn't say. Roughly about five miles from our destination."

Melissa stopped in her tracks. "Five miles of this? It'll be daybreak before we could make five miles in this jungle."

Brett kept walking. "I'm sure five miles is nothing for a fearless reporter." He pushed through some heavy photinia bushes and out of sight.

Melissa looked around, but the terrain looked the same in all directions. Dark and dense. She took quick steps in the direction Brett had disappeared.

She pushed through the bushes and into a clearing. "Five more miles," she mocked him, dropping onto one of the ornate benches at the edge of the rose garden.

"Roughly," he answered lightly, unable to hide his amusement. He motioned for Melissa to follow him to the bronzed fountain that sat in the center of the garden. "Might as well start here."

He took the shovel from her and begin to dig. His hands moved quickly, the damp dirt giving way to the sharp metal and the force of his strength. He dug a trench around the fountain, about two feet deep and a foot wide.

The night was chilly, but beads of perspiration dotted his brow. He stopped and took off his coat, tossing it across a nearby rosebush.

"Looks like this was a sorry guess," he announced, stopping to lean on the shovel. "Might as well finish here and move on." He tossed shovels full of loose dirt back into the hole. "We'll have to leave it just like we found it. If Sylvia suspects anyone was here, she'll have this place guarded like the White House. I'll never be able to sneak in."

A noise sounded in the brush. Melissa spun around, her heart slamming against her ribs.

"Relax. Probably just a raccoon," Brett offered, trying to assuage her fears. "It's only the two-legged creatures we need to be careful of."

But she noticed he kept an eye peeled in the direction of the sound. He worked quickly, pounding the soil down with the shovel until it was just as even as it had been before he'd started digging. Then he raked up a mound of pine straw and spread it over the dirt, piling it up around the fountain.

Melissa used her foot to help, covering their tracks until it was almost impossible to tell the ground had been touched.

"Well, what do you think, reporter lady? What's the next most likely place to hide a diary?"

"I don't know." She studied the layout of the garden in the moonlight. It looked different at night. Shadows played across the small white statues and decorative benches, giving them a spiritlike quality. Almost alive. Almost ready to whisper their dead owner's secrets.

"I'd say that statue of the wood nymph. See how her right hand is stretched out, like she's showing you something? I'd try there. About a foot out. Right where she's pointing."

"It's as good a place as any."

Brett began digging again, his arms moving in an easy, almost hypnotic rhythm. Hypnotic until the second the soft clinking sound met their ears.

He stopped and then pushed the shovel deeper. It sounded again. The touch of metal on metal.

Melissa fell to her knees, frantically clawing through soil. Brett joined her, but she found it first. She wrapped her fingers around it, pushing the dirt away until she could pull it up and into the light.

A can. That was all. An empty can, bent and mangled. Disappointment rose up in the dust to choke her. She handed it to Brett.

He crushed it in his hands and hurled it through the darkness and into the bushes that bordered the garden, cursing the night, the shovel and the lying nymph before he picked up the shovel and started filling the hole.

Melissa sat on one of the benches. It was past mid-
night, and she was bone tired. She'd spent the day and
the better part of the night in this garden. If there was
a diary here, it wasn't meant to be found.

She longed to return to the cabin, to stretch out in the
comfortable bed. They should go. Brett was standing
there doing nothing, as useless as the stupid statue she'd
chosen to believe in.

"This is a waste of time," she complained. "We can't
dig up a whole garden on some whim of yours. There
might not even be a diary. And if there is, it might not
tell us a darn thing."

"Shh." He put his finger to his lips in warning. She
started to complain, but something in his eyes made her
think again.

She waited. And listened. There was only the sound
of the wind. No. There it was. A laugh. High-pitched,
carrying in the breeze. "Is that coming from the
house?"

"I don't think so. Can you find your way to the car?"

"No." She'd followed Brett through a jumbled maze
of bushes, pine trees and undergrowth. And she had no
intention of taking off through there alone. "We'll both
go." She started to grab the tools.

Brett took the shovel and started packing down the
dirt, his arms flying, smoothing it as he went.

Melissa worked with him, praying whoever it was
would just turn around and head to the house. Surely
they would. It was late. Too late for a woman to be
strolling in the garden alone.

Melissa listened, holding her breath. This wasn't what
she wanted to hear. A man's voice, crisp and deep, carried over the creakings of the wind. Her insides quaked.

There were at least two people, and they were coming closer.

"We've got to get out of here, Brett."

"Get in the bushes, Melissa. Hide and keep still. No matter what happens, don't come out."

"I'm not going without you."

"Get out of here, Melissa. Now, while you can. This is my battle." Even in whispers, the urgency came through.

But she couldn't leave him. If he had to finish, then she had to help. With deft movements, she spread pine straw, covering the tracks of the shovel as they had done before. Her breath was coming in jagged gasps, but she pushed her hands to work faster. "Come on, Brett. This is good enough."

The voices were almost on them now. Brett slid the tools into the thick photinia at the edge of the garden and darted into the dense shrubbery, pulling Melissa behind him. They lay on their stomachs on the damp ground, listening and waiting.

"The garden's lovely in the moonlight, Sylvia. I don't know why you didn't want to walk out here with me."

Melissa stretched her neck, but it was no use. She could see nothing. But that voice. Smooth, persuasive. She'd heard it somewhere before.

She studied Brett's profile, the firm set of his jaw only inches from her own. Every line in his face was drawn tight. But it was anger, not fear, that was tearing him apart.

"I do appreciate your coming over tonight. It's been so hard on me since Jason's death. Especially here, in the garden."

"I wanted to come. I worry about you. You can't be too careful, not with that brother-in-law of yours still on the loose."

Mosher. It was him. That voice. It had to be. And just as she'd expected, Sylvia was playing him like a fine guitar, strumming a ballad of innocence and sensuality that he was all too willing to believe.

Unless Brett was the one who... No. She'd made a mistake three years ago. But not this time. She reached for the comfort of Brett's hand. He wrapped his fingers tightly around hers. He met her gaze, and the concern mirrored there said it all. This time she'd chosen well.

"Surely Brett's out of the area by now. I expect he's back in the north woods, playing that macho wilderness game he likes so much," Sylvia crooned sweetly.

"I wouldn't count on that. He had only one thing on his mind in the hospital. He planned to come back here and find Jason's diary. Remember, he even tried to convince me that you had killed Jason."

"Do you think there really is a diary?"

"There could be. Those letters. The ones you were supposed to mail to Brett in Wyoming. Do you still have them?"

"Yes. They're in my room, but they don't make any sense. Whatever Jason was trying to say was lost somewhere in that confused mind of his."

She felt the tight squeeze of Brett's hand, and she knew what he was thinking. The code existed. It was just that they didn't have all the clues. The missing pieces were hidden away in Sylvia's bedroom.

But there was no time to gloat over their small success.

"Where did this come from?"

Melissa held her breath.

"I have no idea. It's just a hunting jacket. Probably belongs to one of the servants."

"Maybe. Or maybe your determined brother-in-law has made his first call."

"Surely not. The servants all know Brett. If he'd been out here someone would have seen him."

"Not in the dark."

"I'm sure he wouldn't come here, Stuart. But don't worry. I'll let Ealey out as soon as we get back to the house. The only time he's seen Brett was after Jason's death, and he didn't take to him at all. Of course, he wasn't taking to anyone then. I had no idea a dog could grieve like that for his master."

"It will take more than a dog to stop Brett Samson."

"Stuart, please, put that gun away. You know how nervous they make me."

Not nearly as nervous as it was making her, Melissa imagined. Her heart was pounding so loudly she was sure they had to hear it.

"You go on back to the house. I want to stay out here a minute. Have a look around. And take this jacket with you."

"No, Stuart. You come to the house with me."

Heavy footsteps moved in their direction. An icy tingle bolted up Melissa's spine, but somehow she managed to hold her breath and lie perfectly still.

The footsteps came closer, and she heard a rustling in the bushes that separated them from the garden. She felt Brett's body grow taut, his muscles straining, readying for attack. He reached into his boot and pulled out a knife.

A hunting knife. Long and curved. And jagged.

The knot in Melissa's stomach bounded to her throat, choking her breath away. She squeezed her eyes shut. Unwilling to see more. Unwilling even to think.

The footsteps moved on.

"I guess you're right, Sylvia. If he had been here, he'd have run when he heard us coming. But we'll turn Ealey loose anyway. The stupid dog never bites anyone but me, but at least he'll make some noise."

Melissa lay by Brett, waiting silently until the footsteps had retreated far up the path, until there was no chance they would be detected. She couldn't look at him. Couldn't face the deadly knife that he clutched in his hand.

But it was only a hunting knife, she told herself. A weapon Brett had brought for their protection. She had to stop this ridiculous trembling and get her emotions under control.

Brett sheathed the knife in his boot before easing out of the bushes. Melissa followed him, and he pulled her to her feet, wrapping her in his arms. She clung to him gratefully. She wasn't sure her legs would hold her up.

And she didn't care to find out. Not when his arms felt this safe.

"Are you all right?"

"Sure," she lied. "Nothing like a close call to get the old heart pumping."

"Then let's get out of here. Get some rest before the real challenge."

"The real challenge?"

"Probably not for a professional like you, Melissa. But breaking into a lady's bedroom will be something new for me."

Chapter Twelve

Melissa looked at her watch for at least the hundredth time. Ten twenty-eight a.m. A little more than thirty minutes before her part in today's espionage escapades was to begin. She opened the leather pouch and began to pack away the bulky rented camera.

She'd been here since eight-thirty, pretending to snap photos of brightly colored pansies and golden mums, shapely evergreens and gurgling fountains. And all in areas safely outside the rose garden.

As far as she was concerned, she'd seen everything there was to see, and none of it had brought them any closer to locating the diary. The only real chance of finding it depended on the success of today's mission.

A mission she had vetoed every step of the way. But here she was, going along with a ridiculous plan that could land them both in jail. Oh, well, she could always do an exposé on prison life. The thought did nothing to relieve her jumpy nerves.

She trudged toward the imposing plantation house. Ten-forty. Brett would have to be close by. Somewhere in the tree line off the back of the house. She scanned the area. Everything was quiet. At least that much was working.

Five more minutes had ticked off the clock by the time she rounded the side of the house. Everything was running according to schedule.

She stopped in her tracks. A strange car pulled out from the drive in front of the house. She could barely see the driver, but he was male with a head full of wavy graying hair.

Mosher. Please don't let it be him, she murmured, knowing all the time it had to be. She swallowed a curse. The one complication they hadn't planned for. But if he was leaving now, it shouldn't change anything.

He gunned the engine. She breathed easier, but not for long. The brakes squealed, and the car came to a screeching halt.

Melissa ducked behind a row of holly bushes. She couldn't risk being seen. Mosher might be a jerk, but he was smart enough to know that the Miss Jackson who'd visited his office had no business snooping around Samson Place.

She shuffled her feet nervously. Ten-fifty.

Mosher revved the engine, but still he didn't pull away. He sat staring at the house as if waiting for something to happen. He pulled up a few feet and stopped again.

Darn. He was looking at the very spot she'd just ducked away from. He must have seen something. Caught a glimpse of her before she had time to duck for cover.

Finally, he eased forward and then took off, disappearing down the curved drive. Melissa straightened her clothes and cautiously moved out from behind the bushes. There was still time. All she needed to do was get inside the house and get Sylvia out of her bedroom.

She held her head and managed a pained expression. She stumbled up the steps, her performance in full swing. There was a good chance the butler was watching her ascent. He definitely didn't miss much.

She knocked once, and he swung the door open. "My goodness, Miss Green, you look ill. Are you all right?"

Her act was obviously working. "No," she whispered in strained tones. "I don't know what it is. I feel faint. I was just coming to tell Mrs. Samson that I won't be able to finish today."

"Here, sit down on the sofa." He led her across the thick carpet, guiding her to a seat. "Can I get you something? Water? Aspirin?"

Ten fifty-five. "Some juice would help. I'm diabetic, and sometimes I just get so caught up in my work I forget to eat. But first, could you get Mrs. Samson? I really must talk to her."

She buried her head in her hands and rocked back as if dizzy. "I told her I'd be finished today, but . . ."

"Of course. You just sit still. I'll be right back. I wish you'd been here a minute or two sooner. You just missed the doctor."

Melissa raised her head enough to watch him scurry up the stairs. Good. The faster the better. Mosher had delayed her just enough to throw their timing off.

She took a quick inventory of the room. There were two windows, both on the east side of the house. That shouldn't be a problem. Brett was coming in the back way. He was planning to climb the big oak and swing from a rope onto the veranda.

Tarzan in his natural habitat. Too bad she had to miss the show.

The minutes ticked away ominously. Melissa was all but ready to go after Sylvia herself when she heard the sultry Southern voice.

"My dear, I'm so sorry to hear you're not feeling well."

She descended the curving staircase as she spoke. A flowing chiffon robe whirled around her ankles, and her hair fell in golden waves around her partially exposed breasts. No wonder Mosher had been reluctant to leave. Any man would have been.

"Thank you," Melissa answered weakly.

Sylvia waltzed over, the emergency taking very little from her Southern belle manner. She took Melissa's hand in hers. "Is there something we can get you? Or someone we can call?"

"Just juice. I think your butler's already getting it. Then I'll be fine."

"Yes, Washington's a dear," she answered, settling herself in a chair opposite Melissa. "Has this happened before?"

"I'm afraid so. When my blood sugar gets low. But it's nothing, really." *Nothing at all,* Melissa added to herself. *But it will be unless I can keep you here.*

Washington returned with a silver tray bearing a tall glass of freshly squeezed orange juice and some slices of apple. He placed it on the table in front of her. "I hope this will help. And if I can get you anything else, just let me know."

Melissa tried to think of something, anything, to send him back into the kitchen. If he was there, he wouldn't be upstairs.

"Well, if it's not too much trouble, could you get me just a tad of sugar for this juice? Immediate energy, you know."

He looked at her quizzically, but he headed in the direction of the kitchen.

Ten fifty-seven. The house was quiet. Too quiet. Even the slightest sound would carry. She had to start talking.

"I know I shouldn't let myself get in this state, but your gardens are so lovely. It's just hard to think of anything else when I'm out there." She sipped the juice. "Especially the rose garden. I can easily see why your late husband loved it so."

"Did I tell you about that?" Sylvia's eyebrows registered surprise. "I guess I must have. He did love it. But it needs some work. We'll be replanting out there soon."

"It looks just about perfect to me like it is, but then I'm sure you know what you want."

"Yes. We plan to do extensive landscaping. You'll have to come back when we finish."

We. Interesting that the grieving widow was already a *we.*

"I'd love to. Actually, I may need to come back tomorrow. I hope that won't be a problem for you." Melissa rocked backwards, resting her head on the cushions. "I'm just so dizzy."

Sylvia handed her the glass of juice. "Here, drink some more of this."

Melissa held it to her lips. She fluttered her eyes, glancing at her watch in between flutters. Ten fifty-nine.

"Could you just show me where the powder room is?"

"Of course, dear. Here, let me help you." Sylvia took her arm.

Melissa clutched it as she got shakily to her feet. She moved slowly, taking two steps before slipping her arm from Sylvia's and crumpling to the floor.

"Washington! Mattie Jean! Hurry. Miss Green's fainted."

Ah, so there was another servant in the house, just as Brett had said. The fainting really was necessary. But difficult. Melissa counted to a hundred, anything to keep her mind busy and her face expressionless. They were all around her, feeling her pulse, pressing a palm to her forehead. And thankfully they were chattering and making a great deal of noise in the process.

"Do you think we should try to get her back on the couch?" Sylvia asked, concern evident in her voice. Melissa felt a reflexive twinge of guilt. She'd never liked to make people worry.

Two strong arms wrapped around her, evidently Washington's. It would have been a lot easier if she could have helped, but she managed to maintain a dead limpness as she was pulled up and deposited on the soft cushions. Then someone slipped her feet out of her shoes and lifted them to the couch, easing her into a reclining position.

"I think we better get a doctor, Miss Sylvia. Do you want me to try Dr. Mosher's car phone number? He couldn't be too far away yet."

Melissa's heart jumped to her throat.

"No, not Stuart," Sylvia answered almost too quickly. "Not with Miss Green being a reporter. You know how he hates publicity."

Welcome to the club, Melissa thought. It's a popular enough sentiment these days. Still, she was thankful he wouldn't be coming back. It would have meant an instant recovery and departure.

Melissa's arm was starting to cramp. She pulled it over and moaned softly, opening her eyes just enough to catch a glimpse of her watch. She'd promised Brett ten minutes. And she planned to deliver. After that he was on his own.

"We might not need to call anyone. She seems to be coming to. Let's give her a minute."

Melissa began to count to herself. She'd go to four hundred. That was it. Four hundred and she'd make a quick recovery and get out of here.

But she never made it to fifty.

A shot rang out, its echo cracking through the house. Melissa jumped to her feet, her heart pounding painfully against her chest.

No one else moved. They stood there and waited as if in a trance. Waited until the next shot rang out. And then another.

Melissa pushed by Sylvia and headed for the steps. Something had gone wrong. Seriously wrong. "Who else is in the house?" she asked, her voice shaky, but her determination strong.

"No one," Sylvia answered, her face ghostly white.

Melissa started up the stairs.

"Sylvia!" A man's voice called out. Melissa backed down. The voice was not Brett's.

"Stuart...is that...you?" Sylvia tried to speak, but the words were long in coming. She dropped to the couch, a shivering, frightened mass.

"It's me," he called down from somewhere out of sight. "Call the police. I just killed your brother-in-law."

Melissa forced her feet to move. Slowly at first. She walked to the front door and opened it. No one even noticed. Washington was on the phone, and Sylvia had

sunk to the couch, wringing her hands and whimper-
ing. Mattie Jean cowered behind her.

Melissa paused. "Not the police, Washington. Call
an ambulance." Shock was settling over her like a sheet
of ice, but she had to make sure Brett had a chance.
"Get an ambulance. He might still be alive."

She stepped outside and gulped for air. The knot that
had started in her chest had dropped to her stomach,
churning sickeningly. They had known there was risk
involved. But not this. Not death.

The world spun crazily around her, but she managed
to stumble to the car. She slid behind the wheel and
started the engine. It was so hard, leaving Brett like this.
Dying among people he hated. But she was without
options. She had to get out now, while she could.

Finally she knew how Brett felt. He was sure Sylvia
had killed his brother, and he couldn't rest until she
paid. Well, now Mosher had killed Brett. But they were
not home free. Not as long as Melissa was alive.

She pulled out of the driveway and onto the empty
highway. The plan had been for her to pick up Brett at
the end of the dirt road where they had parked last
night. He was supposed to be there waiting for her with
the missing letters in hand.

But he wouldn't be there now.

She turned down the road anyway, following some
part of her brain that wouldn't accept what had just
happened. She drove slowly, her eyes searching the
surrounding woods for some sign that it had all been a
mistake. For some sign of a tall, rugged man striding
confidently through a clearing, a smile of satisfaction
on his face.

She stopped in the same place they'd stopped last
night. Brett had been so sure they could pull this off. He

was certain he could get into the house without being seen. How could he miss if Melissa had all the inside help nursing her? But they hadn't counted on Mosher.

He'd driven away. Melissa had watched him disappear down the driveway. But something must have alerted him, must have made him suspicious enough to return to the house and sneak around back.

And she might have been that something. A movement, a flash of color. Something unusual that caught his eye as she ducked behind the holly bushes.

Timing. It was a capricious lover.

Timing had saved her life when Brett had pushed her away from the exploding car. Timing had let her arrive at her apartment precious minutes after her would-be murderer, the paint still wet and dripping. It had let her move an inch to the left of a flying knife with her name on it.

It had let Brett down.

Her spirits careened in a downward spiral. Images of Brett lying in a pool of blood threatened to rob her of the ability to think, to make rational decisions. Her head dropped to the steering wheel as her body slumped forward, giving in to overpowering grief.

Slowly, her strength began to return. She stepped out of the car. She had to have air.

Something moved behind her. She whirled.

"Brett! It's you." She shook her head vigorously, but he didn't disappear. "It's really you." She rushed toward him, falling into him, wrapping him in her arms. Tears rolled down her cheeks, but she was laughing with relief.

Brett caught her in his arms, whirling her around until they fell to the ground in a tangle of arms and legs. "Now this is what I call a welcome." He caught her lips with his, kissing her over and over. Kissing her lips, her nose, her teary eyes.

"I thought you were dead. There were shots. And Mosher..."

"Yeah, Mosher, the man of the hour. There to protect the widow. And her millions. No wonder he was so willing to believe I was a raving lunatic. He was already sleeping with my accuser, or at least working on it."

"Well, you have to admit Sylvia is pretty convincing. And beautiful. But what happened? How did you get away?"

"Get in the car. I'll tell you all about it while we're putting some miles between us and this place."

Brett ushered her to the rented Chevy, then climbed in himself. The motor turned over with a touch of the key, and he accelerated quickly, heading down the dirt road and away from the house, but keeping a close eye on the rearview mirror.

"So," Melissa urged, as he pulled onto the main highway. "What happened? How did you get away?"

Brett loosened his grip on the wheel, reaching one hand over to encircle hers. "I was in the room, going through drawer after drawer. Makeup, jewelry, cards and letters, everything but what I wanted."

"So you didn't find Jason's letters?"

"No. That's the worst part of this whole mess. I've alerted everybody and come away empty-handed. I'll never be able to get in the house now. Not until I'm cleared of their trumped-up psychiatric charges."

And new charges. Like breaking and entering. But this was probably not a good time to mention those.

"Anyway," he continued, "I thought I heard someone in the hall. Not much, just the creakings of the old house with the weight of movement. I headed for the window that opened onto the veranda. I was crawling out when he saw me. I fell through and down onto the porch floor, rolling toward the banister. By the time he got to the window I was already going over the edge, sliding down the rope to the ground."

"But the shots. There were three of them."

"Yeah. He thought the first one hit me. The other two were just for good measure."

Melissa shivered, a cold chill washing across her. She scooted closer, needing Brett's warmth. He wrapped his arm around her, pulling her over to snuggle against him. "I fell to the ground in feigned agony. You're not the only person around here who can act, you know."

"But how did he miss you three times?"

"Who knows? Maybe he's a bad shot. But I didn't exactly make it easy for him. I rolled behind a tree after the first miss. Then when he shot again, I got up and ran, throwing myself to the ground behind one of the cupid fountains, like I could go no further. He shot again, and that time it was close. Close enough I felt the heat. I grabbed my heart and rolled over, rolling the last three feet into the tree line, before stopping to lie dead still."

"That's when he yelled for Sylvia to call the police. He said he'd killed you."

"But he didn't. I can't die yet. I have too much unfinished business."

"Sylvia?" she interjected. "I admit, I had my doubts at first. She's so...fragile. I didn't believe it possible that she could actually kill someone."

"Don't feel bad. No one else did, either. That's how I ended up in a straitjacket."

"She definitely has Mosher sucked in by her little scheme. After today you must be more determined than ever to prove her guilt."

"I am." He nuzzled his chin atop her head, pulling her closer, into the crook of his arm. "But that's not the unfinished business I have on my mind right now."

Melissa snuggled contentedly. She didn't have to ask what he meant.

The time flew as they headed to the cabin. They didn't talk much. They didn't need to. The morning had taken its emotional toll, and for now just being together was enough.

Melissa was almost asleep when Brett pulled into the service station to fill up with gas. She opened her eyes and watched him. She'd never known anyone like him. Never known anyone who had the effect on her he did.

He was ruggedly handsome. Strong, but firm and lean, with confidence in his every move. He was sturdy, dependable. A rock that would be there when you needed him.

He finished pumping the gas and then strode over to the outdoor pay phone. She watched him dial a number from memory. He stood in the bright afternoon sunshine, his face lined in deep concentration.

She noticed his shoulders first, noticed the way they straightened, his whole body coming to attention. Then she saw it on his face. Saw his mouth split from side to side in a dashingly brilliant smile. He hadn't said a word, but whatever he'd heard on the other end of the line had to be great news.

He swung his body into the car with a lightness of mood Melissa had never seen in him. He slid a rough hand under her chin and tilted her face upward. He touched his lips to hers, deliciously. Just a touch. A touch of heaven.

"Eric's back in the States." His excitement echoed in every word. "There was a message on our answering machine. He's flying to New Orleans in the morning." He kissed her again, this time slow and penetrating, taking her breath away with his thoroughness. "We'll see a judge. And then, my pretty lady, we'll finish up this business once and for all."

His joy was contagious. Except for one nagging thought that chipped away at Melissa's share of the excitement. When the business was finished, Brett would return to Wyoming.

MELISSA HUGGED her arms around her, pushing off the cold night air as she walked along the water's edge. Moonlight filtered through the bare branches of the cypress trees, painting streaks of gold along the slowly moving waters. Tranquil and beautiful. No wonder this had always been her haven in times of trouble.

But it would never be again. Now it would be too full of memories. Too full of Brett. She heard footsteps behind her, but she kept her face directed toward the water.

Everything was working out for the best. Now they would both be able to go on with normal lives. They'd been riding tumultuous waves on a sinking ship. And the trip had nearly claimed both their lives. It was time to move on.

She and Brett had shared a special bond, but the bond was all based on the here and now. It didn't reach deep enough, didn't touch their real lives. In truth, Brett hated reporters, felt nothing but contempt for everything she stood for.

And she still knew far too little about who he really was to even think about a possible future together. Her life was sometimes dangerous, just as Brett had said. But it was ordered. And purposeful.

Brett was still the mystery man. For one thing, there was Ellen Lane. He'd lost someone he loved, he'd said, and it had changed his life forever. The sadness had still been there in his voice and in his eyes. If that love still claimed his heart, there'd be no room for anyone else.

Brett stepped behind her and encircled her waist with his strong arms. "I can't begin to thank you for all you've done."

"There's no reason to. I only did what I wanted to do. What I felt was right."

He buried his warm lips in the curve of her neck, trailed kisses downward then up to her earlobe. Heat flooded through her, the flames licking their way to every part of her body.

He pulled her around to face him. His gaze raked over her, devoured her with the same intensity his body had during their night of love.

Their night of love. One night to last an eternity. She wanted to lose herself in him again, feel the sweetness of satisfying his every desire. The ecstasy of having him do the same for her.

"This is hard for me, Melissa." He twisted his fingers through a lock of her hair. "I've never been comfortable with this sort of thing."

"Then don't try, Brett. I'm not asking anything of you." She stepped away. It would be easier if his lips were not so close. "This has been an emotional week for both of us," she continued, striving for an outward calm she didn't feel. "We needed each other. In every way. But I'm not naive enough to believe it was anything more than just what it was.''

"That's just it, Melissa. I don't know what it was. I only know how it felt. How just being with you feels." He traced her cheek with a touch as gentle as the morning mist.

"Not now, Brett." She couldn't deal with any more emotional trauma. The last few days had left her far too vulnerable. "It's not the time. Not for either of us."

"It's past time for me, Melissa. Years past time."

His voice trembled. Whatever he had to say was not easy for him. She studied his face in the moonlight and lost herself in the depths of his eyes.

"I haven't had much experience with love. Not unless you count the family kind. To be honest with you, I'm not at all sure I have it in me."

She opened her mouth to protest. There was no reason to deny the love he'd already confessed. She wanted no part of a relationship built on deceptions. He silenced her with a gentle finger on her lips.

"Something's happened to me this week. In the middle of bombings and knifings, fever and gunshots. I'm not sure what it is, but I do know one thing. The other night, when I realized how close I'd come to losing you, something exploded inside me. Suddenly *not* losing you was the most important thing in the world."

He lowered his face, touching the tip of her nose and then her lips with the lightest of kisses. She leaned against him. He was like a drug, weakening her resistance, lulling her into a perilous euphoria.

But this time she would not give in to her traitorous longings. She'd played games with her heart once before and she'd lost. She wouldn't make that mistake

again. She lifted her head and focused on the spark that
smoldered in his eyes.

"I care about you, Brett. More than I ever dreamed
possible. I won't deny it. But we have no past together.
We only know the here and now. It's barely a beginning. It takes time to develop the kind of trust that re-
lationships are built on. Trust and total honesty."

He loosened his grip on her and raised his eyebrows
inquiringly. "I thought baring my soul was being honest."

"There are a lot of things you don't know about me,
Brett. And some of the things you do know, you can't
accept. Like who and what I stand for. And there are
things I don't know about you."

"No beating around the bush, Melissa. Just spit it
out," he countered flippantly, seemingly reading her
mind once more. A sudden irritation chipped away at
his composure, chilling the air between them with frosty
gusts. "What is it you've heard about the dangerous
and crazy Brett Samson that has you worried?"

She'd said she wanted honesty. Now she wasn't sure.
Doubts rose up to choke her. Things she'd managed to
push aside during their lovemaking, during their shared
dangers at Samson Place. Pushed aside but obviously
not buried. The drugs she'd found in his room. The
newspaper accusations. His confession of lost love.

She met his threatening gaze. "For starters, tell me
about Ellen Lane."

Chapter Thirteen

Brett stared at Melissa coldly, every muscle in his body clenched. The anger contorted his face and burned reproachfully in his eyes.

A silent warning sounded in her brain. This was a totally different Brett from the one she'd lived with the past few days. She didn't really know this man at all.

"How did you find out about Ellen Lane?" He forced the words through clenched teeth.

"I looked it up. It's public knowledge." She fought the suspicions mounting inside her; fought to keep her voice calm.

"It was twelve years ago. You had to dig damn deep."

"That's not true. I was looking up Mosher. I just stumbled across the story." She wouldn't be intimidated by him. There was nothing dishonorable about her actions. Or her questions.

"Ah, yes. The mark of a good reporter. Uncover any hidden filth," he quipped sarcastically.

"No, not filth. Truth. I've risked a lot for you, Brett Samson. The truth is all I'm asking in return."

"Okay, Melissa. Have a seat." He motioned to the wooden picnic table tucked away under the trees. "I'll give you all the scandal in glorious color."

Melissa dropped to the bench. Brett didn't join her. He paced, his fists clenched, the veins in his face stretched into tight lines.

"I dated Ellen Lane off and on all through high school. Nothing really serious. Then, about midway through our senior year, she broke it off. Said she was seeing someone else. An older guy she didn't want her mother to know about."

"That must have upset you very much."

Brett spun around to face her. "No, it didn't. And don't use that patronizing, psychiatric tone with me. I had enough of that from Mosher."

Melissa nodded in agreement. Brett was right. She'd asked for his story. She owed it to him to let him tell it without interruption.

"A bunch of the guys and I went out to Lucky's on graduation night. It wasn't much of a place. A few pool tables and cheap beer."

He moved to the other side of the picnic table and propped his foot up on the bench. "When we got there we saw Ellen and her boyfriend standing at the edge of the parking lot. I'd planned to walk right past, but she called my name. I waved and walked on in with the others."

Brett ran his fingers nervously through his hair. "Her eyes were red and swollen. I couldn't get it off my mind. I went outside alone, just to make sure she was all right."

Melissa shivered, suddenly cold through and through. Not from the temperature but from the frosty pain that iced Brett's words.

"I saw him hit her. Hard. Across the face. I didn't even think. I just rushed right in like the young fool I was."

Like the brave soul he still was, Melissa acknowledged silently. Like he'd done with her. Throwing himself in the path of a bomb to push her out of the way. She was the fool for making him relive this pain.

"The guy and I ended up in a fight," he continued. "He won, hands down. We *rich* boys never learned to fight dirty. He broke a beer bottle over my head."

Melissa reached for his hand. He jerked it away. "Nothing to get sentimental about, Melissa. It was just a fight in a dark parking lot. Not nearly as sordid as the papers made it sound, but then you reporters have a knack for that sort of thing, don't you?"

Melissa got up from the bench. "I've heard enough, Brett. Let's just drop the rest. It's been a long day."

"Oh, don't go now, reporter lady. We're just getting to the good part."

He lowered himself to the bench. "Ellen was drunk. I told her to get in my car and I'd drive her home. But we never made it. Somewhere along the way I passed out, a concussion from the blow. We wound up wrapped around a tree."

Brett buried his head in his hands. "Ellen died, and her mother wanted someone to blame. She didn't have a leg to stand on, but there was one overzealous reporter, a local, who didn't see it that way. We made the headlines every day."

"Mistakes happen, Brett. That one was unfortunate. But you were found innocent."

"Right. Simple mistakes. Only my mother couldn't handle having people she thought were her friends marching in the road by our house demanding her son go to jail."

Brett got up from the bench and stood staring into the darkness. "She had a stroke the day the police came to my house and dragged me off in handcuffs. She never fully recovered." His voice broke, and he knotted his trembling hands into fists. "She died a few weeks later."

Melissa's heart went out to him. She couldn't keep silent. "That must have been terrible for you."

"It was rough, all right, on Jason and me. It was a lot harder on my dad. He suffered a fatal heart attack before the year was out."

"I'm sorry, Brett. I didn't know. The papers didn't say..."

"No, the ambitious young reporter had grown tired of us by then and moved on to another town. To find other lives to ruin. Or maybe he was fired. I never knew which. At that point, it really didn't matter much."

Melissa controlled the rising tears. "You lost so much."

Brett shrugged. "It was a long time ago."

True. Brett had probably dealt with the death of his parents a long time ago, but now he'd lost again. This time his brother was dead. The only family he had left.

And once again, he was laying the blame on himself. He hadn't taken the first letter seriously. By the time he got the last letters, it had been too late.

And once again, she'd let Robert Galliano sneak into her life, adding doubt where none should have existed.

Trust. She talked a good story. That wasn't enough. She had to learn to put the past behind her. She had to learn to trust her intuition and good judgment. Even in matters of the heart.

Brett turned and walked toward the cabin without a backward glance.

A tear slid down her cheek as she watched him go. "Why couldn't I just trust my feelings?" she whispered into the silence of the night. "Or even my heart?"

MELISSA ROLLED on some lipstick and then added a touch of blush to her cheeks. It helped a little, but her eyes still showed signs of her sleepless night. Sleepless until the wee hours of the morning when she must have slept far too soundly. She hadn't heard Brett leave for New Orleans and his important rendezvous with his partner.

She ran a brush through her dark curls. He'd taken the raggedy pickup truck, telling Cotile he'd have it back to her sometime that night. He and Cotile were both sure the battered vehicle would make the trip.

Why not, Cotile had answered when Melissa had questioned her about it later in the morning. It had made over a hundred thousand miles before.

But at least he was coming back. After seeing his anger last night, Melissa had feared he'd never return to the cabin. Not once his passport to freedom arrived at the airport.

She grabbed her coat and headed out the door. She'd promised Marvin she'd come in for questioning. This was as good a time as any. She definitely didn't want to wander around in the empty cabin the rest of the day.

It was only a little after noon, and already she was going stir-crazy.

Besides, she knew Marvin. If she didn't make it in soon, he'd be at the cabin looking for her.

The long drive provided time to think and to worry. Melissa flicked on the radio, but neither music nor the endless raving of an arrogant radio host could put Sylvia and Samson Place out of her mind.

Brett was confident the worst was over. He and Eric would go to a judge and present evidence to prove Brett was a sane and respectable businessman. Then Brett would be free to search the rose garden to his heart's content. After all, he was half owner of Samson Place.

Melissa had serious doubts about any of that. This was New Orleans. The Big Easy. Brett had apparently forgotten how slowly the wheels of justice turned here. It might take him days to even see a judge. By then, the diary could easily have fallen into the hands of the enemy.

Sylvia had already talked about relandscaping the rose garden. As far as Melissa was concerned, relandscaping translated into digging it up. Digging up as much as she had to in order to find the diary. Find it and destroy it.

She searched her mind, reliving every step she'd made through the garden. There had to be something she and Brett had overlooked. Some clue. Some thing or some person who could shed a little light on where Jason might have hidden his incriminating revelations.

Mosher was out. That was for sure. Sylvia had him so wrapped around her dainty little fingers, he wouldn't be able to see the truth if it came gift wrapped.

There was Washington, but they'd get nothing there, either. He was loyal to his mistress. Loyal to the core, unless Melissa missed her guess. And as far as Mattie Jean was concerned, she didn't appear to have a clue about the clandestine goings-on.

That left Ealey. If only he could talk, solving the puzzle would be a done deal.

Melissa's mind clicked into high gear. Ealey couldn't talk. But old Zeke could. And did. He'd told her about the plants in a lot more detail than she'd cared to know. If she could get him started talking about Jason, he might be just as verbose.

And there was a chance he knew something. Slight, but worth a try. He would have been the most likely person to see Jason digging around in the garden or even to notice a place where the dirt had been freshly turned.

Melissa pressed on the accelerator. A stop at Samson Place wouldn't be much out of the way.

THREE HOURS LATER, her plan of action well thought out, she pulled into the tree-lined drive. She'd bypass the house and go directly to the rose garden. Washington would be sure to notice her car and report it to Sylvia, but that shouldn't matter. She'd told Sylvia yesterday that she hadn't quite finished.

Melissa grabbed her camera and bounded from the car and down the brick path to the garden. A loud barking drew her up short. Ealey was out and on the prowl, just like Mosher had suggested to Sylvia.

Melissa slowed her pace but kept moving toward the garden. He'd let her pet him that first day. Of course,

Zeke had been around then to keep him in line. Still, with any luck, he'd consider her a friend.

He ran up to her, yelping steadily. Dogs sense fear. She'd always heard that. She just hoped this one could be fooled. She put out her hand. He sniffed it thoroughly before enveloping it in his hot, pink tongue.

"Hello, pretty boy. That's right. You just keep licking. Just like we're old friends. You keep licking and I'll try to stop shivering in my shoes, even though you are the size of a small horse." Melissa crooned the words like a love song, and the excited dog settled down, trotting along beside her as she continued down the path, rounding the corner to the rose garden.

The potent smell of fresh-dug soil provided the first warning of what lay ahead. But nothing could have prepared her for the sight.

She stood still, drinking it all in, stunned by the total devastation. Rosebushes had been dug up and thrown in a huge pile to wilt in the afternoon sun. Statues had been ripped from their concrete slabs, and expensive wrought-iron garden furniture had been pushed into the bushes.

"Miss Green!"

The voice startled her. And the name. It was so hard to remember aliases. She spun around to find Mattie Jean glaring at her.

"Miss Sylvia wants you to come to the house. She needs to see you. At once."

A smile parted the young woman's lips as she emphasized the last words. It was probably a real treat for her to be giving instead of receiving that message.

Melissa hesitated. She could opt not to follow Mattie Jean's commands. She could hightail it to the car and see how fast she could get out of here. But if she did, she'd give up all chance of talking to Zeke and of finding out if the diary had already been found.

"Wait, Mattie, I'll walk up with you." She'd take no chances. Even if Sylvia had found out that the story for *Southern Homes and Gardens* was just a ruse to get on the grounds, she had too much sense to try anything in front of the hired help.

Mattie Jean flipped her long black hair out of her eyes. "Okay, but you better hurry. Miss Sylvia's real upset today. She's biting everybody's head off, and I think you're next."

Fine. Melissa could handle a little chewing out. It was knives and guns that made her nervous. She placed her camera on one of the overturned benches, careful to give herself a reason to return.

Sylvia was waiting when they entered the foyer, her hair pulled back in a severe knot, her face pale even through the layers of makeup. She greeted her guest coldly and went right for the jugular.

"I want you off my place at once."

"Of course, Mrs. Samson. I'm sure we have enough material to run a beautiful layout of your grounds. I'm just thankful we were able to get pictures of the rose garden before it was destroyed," Melissa added innocently.

"I've changed my mind about the story. You are not to print one word about Samson Place. Is that clear?"

Perfectly clear. But nothing else was. Sylvia's hands had started to shake, and her voice had cracked while delivering her ultimatum. Something was definitely up.

"I'm sorry for whatever I've done to upset you. But we'll abide by your decision. It's the magazine's policy.

I'll get my things from the rose garden and leave at once.''

Melissa extended her hand. To her surprise, Sylvia took it.

"No. It's nothing you've done. It's personal." She clung to Melissa's hand for just an instant before letting her fingers grow limp. She walked to the door and opened it. "But you must go." She glanced at her watch. "Right away."

"Yes. Of course. It's your home. I'm only a guest."

Melissa took the steps two at a time. She'd get out as quickly as she could, but first she had to make a couple of stops. She headed for the rose garden. She was sure someone from the house would be watching. If she went in any other direction, they'd be on her tail in nothing flat.

She retrieved the camera and cut through the bushes to the combination greenhouse and workshop. With any luck she'd be able to catch Zeke working there. It would be her last chance to pick his brain.

Her last chance to help Brett. If Sylvia hadn't found the diary yet, she would soon. At least half of the garden had already been unearthed.

Melissa opened the door to the greenhouse. "Zeke. Are you in here?" She kept her voice low, not wanting it to carry beyond the glass walls. She waited quietly, but there was no answer. Keeping her eyes peeled for movement, she wandered down a row of lush plants that led to the workshop entry.

"Zeke." Her voice echoed back to her from the wooden beams. She went inside. The workshop was dark and smelled of chemicals and fertilizer. Her eyes slowly adjusted to the lack of light as she made her way through shelves that were cluttered with clay pots and hand tools, old rags and watering pots, shears and long, sharp knives. But there was no sign of the friendly gardener.

She couldn't wait any longer. She started toward the open door. A small metal cross caught her eye. She picked it up, running her fingers along the ornate carving. So strange to find something like that tossed among the clutter.

"Were you looking for me?"

Melissa's heart leaped to her throat as the husky male voice broke into her thoughts. She spun around.

"Sorry, I didn't mean to frighten you." The gardener flashed his toothy grin.

"I guess I'm just a little jumpy these days," she answered in her friendliest tone.

"Yeah, we all are. What with all the outsiders coming in wreckin' the place. I'm glad Mr. Jason's not here to see this. Of course if'n he was, t'wouldn't be happening, now, would it?"

"No. I suppose not." Melissa agreed. "Tell me, Zeke, do you know anything about a diary that Jason was writing in before his death?"

"You mean do I know where it is? No. That's the same question Miss Sylvia and that nosy doctor friend of hers asked me. 'Course I wouldn't have told them, no way. Not even if I knew."

"Then you didn't see him bury anything at all?"

"No, ma'am. Nothing. How come you asking questions like that? Are you some kind of policewoman?"

"No. I was just interested. But do me a favor, will you? Don't mention anything about our conversation to Miss Sylvia."

"No, ma'am. I'm not tellin' her nothin'. Not the way she's acting now. Tearing up my garden without asking me a thing about it. Worked for the Samson family for twenty years. That's the thanks I get."

"No wonder you're upset," Melissa consoled. She placed the cross on the worktable. "Such a beautiful piece," she noted, slinging her camera bag over her shoulder.

"Yeah. Mr. Jason had that special made. Goes on the grave of his old hunting dog. Blew off the other night during the storm. Got to get it back up, though. Mr. Jason loved old Beauregard. He'd want him to have his marker."

Beauregard. Beauregard's cross.

Excitement ran rampant through Melissa's senses. The pieces were suddenly falling together in beautiful harmony, but she struggled to maintain a deceptive calm. "I hope they haven't dug up Beauregard's grave with the new landscaping project."

"Landscaping. Huh. That's not what I'd call it. They haven't touched old Beauregard's grave yet, but t'wouldn't surprise me none if they did. No respect for nothing."

Grammar might not be Zeke's long suit, Melissa decided, but he sure had a way of speaking the truth. She pressed further. "I think I might have seen his grave yesterday," she lied. "Isn't it in the rose garden?"

"No, but it's close. Beauregard liked the shade, and that's where Mr. Jason put him to rest. Right under that big oak tree just to the left of the garden entrance."

"He sounds like he was a very thoughtful man. I'm sure Miss Sylvia's still upset over his death," Melissa baited. "Yesterday she was as sweet as she could be, but today she demanded I get off the property."

"Yeah, she gets in those moods. 'Specially when that doctor fellow's been hangin' around. Like you say, though, she can be nice. Why, just today she decided to give everybody a couple of days off. Starting tonight."

"That is nice. It must be a special occasion."

"No, that's the strange part. She said she and the doc were going to a concert tonight and then they'd be coming back here. Said he'd be staying through tomorrow. Some kind of research project, according to her." The derision was evident in his voice and his expression. "I reckon we all know what kind of research he'll be doing tonight."

She tended to agree with Zeke's assessment, but right now she had more important things on her mind. She thanked him for all the help he'd given her the last few days and made a quick exit. There were plans to be made.

MELISSA SAT in her car at the edge of the shopping center parking lot as the sun colorfully teased the horizon. Once more she mentally checked off her supplies. A steak for Ealey. A shovel. A flashlight.

Nothing was missing. Nothing except Brett. But there hadn't been time to drive to the cabin. The move had to be made while Sylvia and her devoted doctor friend were at the concert.

There would be no real danger. She knew right where to dig. Within thirty minutes after she parked the car, she could have the diary in her hands.

The biggest problem would be retracing the wooded maze Brett had guided her through the other night. But she could park in the exact same place. And tonight would be bright and cloudless. She could use the stars as a . . .

A compass. The one item she'd forgotten.

And she'd definitely be better off with a real one. Her knowledge of astronomy only got her a *C* at LSU, and that had been years ago.

She made one last trip into the busy discount department store and then headed to Samson place. The butterflies were converging by the hundreds now, gathering in the pit of her churning stomach, but she drove with a steady hand and foot. Tonight was too important. She could let nothing stand in her way.

This would be for Brett. He'd been angrier last night than she'd ever seen him. Angry and hurt. And with just cause. He'd given her every reason to trust him. But when the chips were down, she'd ignored all those reasons. Her insecurities had won out, and she'd looked for any excuse not to listen to her heart.

True, he hated reporters, but if anyone ever had a reason to, it was Brett. He'd encountered the worst kind. The ones who'd sell their own souls for a story. But they were the minority, and with time and love, she could have convinced him of that. Now they'd never have the time. Or the love.

She turned down the dark road that led to the back of the garden. There was only one thing she could do for Brett. A parting gift. Something to remember her by. Tonight she'd lay the diary in his hand.

Melissa slowed the car, pulling onto the shoulder of the narrow road. She gathered her supplies and dropped them to the other side of the fence before carefully squirming through the barbed wire.

A strange fear crawled across her skin. The woods were so different now that she was here alone. An owl called from a nearby tree, and a large armadillo wandered aimlessly across her path. She shifted the shovel to her right hand so she could brush away a hungry mosquito that had decided to feast on her right shoulder.

The ground shifted beneath her. Her right foot slid and settled in a hidden hole. She pitched forward, balancing herself with the outstretched shovel. Pain shot through her leg, radiating upward from the twisted ankle.

She dropped to the ground and rubbed the throbbing ankle through the heavy woolen sock. A moan escaped her lips, but there was nothing she could do. She eased to a standing position. She had to move on.

The limp slowed her progress. She pushed herself harder. She had to ignore the pain. Time was too precious to waste.

After what seemed like hours, Melissa spotted the dense photinia bushes. She eased through them and into the garden. But walking here was even more difficult. The newly dug soil lay in loose mounds, and footing was never sure. She dragged the aching foot, each step generating sharp pains that shot mercilessly up her leg.

Nothing was going according to plan. Nothing except Ealey. She could hear him now, rushing through the bushes, his loud barking dominating the night. She dangled the steak in front of her as soon as he came into view. He quieted immediately, eager to take the bait from his new friend.

He lunged for it just as she heaved it forward, sending it flying over the thick border of shrubs. He disappeared right behind it.

Melissa limped toward the tree. She started at the base, then extended the light outward, moving the flashlight in ever widening circles until it illuminated the grave. The uniform mound of dirt was evident even without the missing marker.

She began digging at once, but the work was slow and excruciatingly painful. She pushed the shovel into the earth with all the force she could muster, biting her lip to hold back the cries of pain.

One shovelful of soil followed another and another until a small mountain started growing at her side. She checked each lump of dirt carefully, using the end of the shovel to search for foreign objects. There was nothing. Just more dirt.

Disappointment mingled with agony. She'd been so sure she'd find the diary. Sure that this time the clue was unmistakable. Beauregard's cross. The dog's grave.

She glanced at her watch. She was running out of time but she couldn't give up yet. She pushed on the shovel.

She was growing weaker. Bearing down with all her strength, she could barely break the hard surface. She took a breath and tried again.

The shovel slid to the right, creating a low clinking sound. She pressed again. The sound grew louder.

Melissa dropped to her knees, directing a circle of light over the spot. A glint twinkled at her.

She sank her hands into the dirt, anticipation pushing away her pain. Her fingers clawed their way around four sharp corners. She dug deeper, her pulses racing as she finally freed the metal container.

She brushed the dirt from the box and raised the fitted lid. With shaking hands, she carefully lifted the leather-bound diary and held it up to the light.

But there was no time for celebrating. Her heart slammed against her chest as a snarling male voice cut through the night.

"I'll take that."

Chapter Fourteen

Melissa spun around. A man stepped from the shadows.

"Hand that to me," he said gruffly, and pointed a silver pistol in her direction.

Mosher. Damn! A few more minutes and she'd have been home free. But at least it was Mosher and not Sylvia who'd discovered her here. He was a sane man. Surely she could reason with him.

"Dr. Mosher, thank God it's you. I have something here I think you and the police will be interested in."

"Do you, my dear?" His voice softened, and his eyes raked over her. He reached for the diary.

She let it go without a fight. It seemed a good idea since he had bullets to back up his demands.

"I can't speak for the police, of course, but I do appreciate your doing the dirty work for me. You've saved me a lot of trouble, delivering yourself and the diary."

"It's not what you think, Dr. Mosher. Sylvia Samson is not what you think." She had to talk fast. Mosher was clearly operating under Sylvia's illusions.

"No, my dear. Sylvia Samson is not what *you* think. But it doesn't really matter now. No one will know what you think. They'll only feel sorry for poor Dr. Mosher, having to kill an intruder." He studied her quietly, his voice as smooth as velvet as he slid into his psychiatrist mode.

She'd figured it all wrong. She should have known Sylvia couldn't have carried out a murder on her own.

"Why so quiet, Miss Bentley, or is it Jackson today? Or perhaps Green? Whatever name you're going by, you do know I have to kill you, don't you?"

Melissa stared at him icily. "Like you killed Jason?"

"Oh, no. That was a work of art. A masterpiece I conducted from beginning to end."

"Jason Samson died of natural causes," she countered, stalling for precious time.

"Ah, that's the beauty of the whole thing. One of the many advantages of a medical degree. I picked up the prescriptions his internist prescribed when he had the flu. It was nothing more than a decongestant, but small doses of chlorpromazine added to his daily medication prolonged the symptoms for weeks. Kept them around until everyone agreed with me that he was merely depressed."

Cold fear gripped Melissa, constricting and squeezing her breath away. Mosher was capable of killing with no remorse. And she was to be his next victim. She had to keep him talking.

"That was brilliant, but I thought Jason died of a heart attack."

"Heart attacks can be planned, my dear. When the time was right, I upped the dosage, bringing on ventricular fibrillation and massive cardiovascular failure."

"Just an untimely death of a good man," Melissa offered. "How convenient for you."

"Yes, and it would have stayed that way if Brett hadn't arrived, determined to stir up trouble." His voice grew hard, his patience clearly wearing thin. "Too bad the bomb missed. I could have taken care of both of you at once, and this nasty thing would have all been over."

Realization swept over her in frightening waves. "Then it was you, not Rocky, all along."

"Yes. But you might call it a combined effort."

Melissa saw the movement from the corner of her eye. First a shadow, then a sweeping glance of blond hair. Brett. Somehow he'd come to the garden, too. Relief surged and then merged with reality. She had to warn him about the gun.

"A combined effort? But Rocky was in jail. He couldn't set a bomb. And he's not standing here with a loaded gun. Not the way you are." She raised her voice a decibel or two.

He smiled tauntingly, then pointed the pistol at her heart. "No, but Rocky and I have shared a long and lucrative friendship. He's the one who introduced me to Boutte."

Brett eased through the bushes, circling closer. She had to keep Mosher talking until Brett could safely make his move. "So you knew who I was when I came to your office?"

"I knew from the moment Brett commandeered you and your car. Or at least shortly thereafter. I had Boutte on his tail even then."

"You were that eager to have him returned to the hospital?"

"To the hospital?" Satirical laughter rolled off his lips. "Not a chance, my dear. His escape was the perfect opportunity to kill him. To silence him forever."

Mosher stepped closer, waving the gun recklessly, obviously enjoying confessing his sins. "We were only after Brett then. Even Boutte didn't recognize you at first as the reporter who'd framed Rocky. Not until he had your license plate checked."

"So the bomb was meant for both of us?"

"Right. You would have been the added bonus. Only Boutte botched the job, leaving the door open for the two of you to escape to your swamp love cabin. It took days to track you down again."

"And Miss Sands, was that part of Boutte's handiwork, too?"

"Yes, at my bidding, of course. Your apartment, as well, though I heard he added some special touches of his own," Mosher added, a malicious chuckle all but smothering his confessions.

Melissa guarded her expression carefully as Brett stepped closer and placed his own gun squarely in Mosher's back.

"Drop the piece, Mosher. Your sick little party's over."

"You won't get away with this, Samson."

"Drop it," he demanded, pushing his gun between Mosher's shoulder blades with enough force to shove him forward. "Now!"

The gun fell from Mosher's hand, landing at his feet. Brett gave it a solid kick, sending it flying into the hole Melissa had dug.

"He has the diary, Brett."

"Toss it to the lady, Mosher. And don't try any funny stuff. There's nothing I'd like better than a reason to pull this trigger."

Mosher followed orders, and Melissa caught the precious book, dropping it inside her shirt for safekeeping.

"Take the diary with my compliments. It won't do you a bit of good. No one will believe any of Jason's absurd insinuations about an affair between Sylvia and me. Why would they take the word of a diagnosed schizophrenic against two upstanding members of the community?"

"There was nothing wrong with my brother, and you know it."

"Of course there was. The evidence is all there in black-and-white. Written down in detail at my office."

"Fine, Mosher. My brother and I are both nuts. It's all there in your records. No one's going to believe me or the diary, so I'll just kill you right now. Kill you and enjoy every minute of watching you die, just like your friend Boutte did with Emily Sands."

Brett moved the gun to the back of Mosher's head. "What do you think, Melissa? Would you like to see his brain or his heart spilled over his silk suit?"

"No. Wait." Mosher was pleading. His body shook and beads of sweat popped out like measles all over his forehead.

"It was Sylvia who planned everything. She killed Jason. I had no idea. Not until it was too late."

"You're pathetic, Mosher." Brett walked over to stand beside Melissa, the gun still pointed directly at the doctor. "A sick wimp of a man who'd hide behind a woman's skirts. You deserve to die."

"No, you've got to believe me." Mosher fell to his knees. "It was Sylvia's idea. She carried out the whole thing from beginning to end. She's blackmailing me. Unless I go along with her, she'll blame the murder on me. But I'll tell the truth, I promise. I'll tell everything. Just don't shoot me."

Tears were running down his cheeks, and his voice was lost in his sobs. "Please, don't shoot."

"Don't shoot him, Brett. There have been too many deaths already."

Melissa turned in the direction of the voice. Sylvia stood at the edge of the garden, ashen, her white robe blending with the pasty color of her face.

Melissa eased toward the gun Brett had kicked away from Mosher, her foot so swollen she could barely walk. Sylvia moved closer, her gaze never leaving her lover's face. A low accusing cry escaped her lips.

Melissa saw it coming, but it happened so fast. There was no time to call out, no time for anything. Ealey bounded from the bushes. He'd heard his mistress cry, and he was her protector.

The huge dog raced forward, hitting Brett squarely in the back of the knees, sending him staggering forward. Mosher lunged, using his right hand to chop the gun from Brett's hand. It flew forward.

Melissa tried to grab it, but Mosher was much closer. He retrieved it with one fatal swoop.

"Good dog, Ealey." Mosher grabbed Melissa's arm and pushed her toward Brett. "Put your hands over your head, both of you."

Melissa obeyed quickly. Brett ignored the order.

"And Sylvia, pull yourself together. Everything's under control. Just look in the hole over there. The one

Miss Bentley was kind enough to dig for us. And pick up the gun.''

Melissa was sure Sylvia would not do as Mosher said. Not after the accusations he'd made against her. But she was wrong. Sylvia stared at Mosher for one brief moment, then walked slowly toward the gun. She picked it up and cradled it in her hands like a newborn baby.

"Why did you kill him?" she demanded.

"We'll talk about it later, Sylvia. There's no time now. You must do as I say."

Sylvia rocked back and forth on her heels, shock and disbelief stretching her fragile control to its limits. Melissa knew she'd heard Mosher's words clearly. Knew he had been willing to place all the blame in her corner. Anything to save his own hide.

"You heard him, Sylvia, with your own ears. He killed your husband," Melissa reminded her gently. If she could help Sylvia get through the shock and anger she was feeling right now, maybe there was enough hidden strength to do what was right.

"Stay out of it." Mosher hurled the threatening words at Melissa.

"You killed him, Stuart. You promised me you wouldn't hurt him." She stepped toward him, holding the gun in front of her. "You said you'd only give him enough medicine to make him drowsy and depressed. Chronically depressed, don't you remember? Then I could get a divorce and keep half of the money. We could have been married then. Half would have been enough, even for us."

"You wanted him dead, Sylvia. You know you did. You wanted the money at any cost. Your exact words," Mosher reminded her, his voice insistent.

She started to weave back and forth, rocking gently on her heels, still cradling the gun in her arms. "You lied to me, Stuart. Lied to me all along. You killed Jason, but you didn't have to. The depression scheme would have worked. We could have walked away from this without a hitch. And without a murder."

"I did what was best for us, my dear. You must believe me. I love you, Sylvia. You can't listen to these people. They just want to destroy us. This woman is an imposter. Brett's lover. Brett doesn't care about you. And he didn't care about Jason. He just wants the Samson money for himself. Now, go back inside and wait. I'll take care of everything."

Sylvia turned toward the house.

"Don't listen to him, Sylvia. He's lying again." Sylvia was their one way out, and Melissa was not about to let her walk away. Not when she held the other loaded gun. "You heard what he said. He said you killed Jason. He doesn't love you. He murdered your husband, and he wants you to go to jail for it."

"Just go in the house, baby. Everything's all right. Call the police. Tell them we heard a noise and that I went out to check on it."

Sylvia moved toward the house slowly, as if in a trance.

Brett stood silently. But Melissa had no intention of giving up without a fight. "How do you know he won't kill you next, Sylvia? He's killing us. We know too much. And now you know too much."

"I told you to keep quiet." Melissa felt Mosher's rough hands as he reached out and grabbed her around the waist. She tried to push away from him, but he locked her in his grip.

"Sylvia, don't to it," she called again. "He'll have to kill you, too."

Sylvia kept walking.

"Okay, little reporter, looks like you'll be the first to die. That way your boyfriend over there can watch."

Sylvia turned around sharply. "Let her go, Stuart."

"I told you to get in the house and call the police. Now do as I say!"

Sylvia straightened her back defiantly. "Not anymore, Stuart. Not anymore." She stared at him coldly and turned and tossed the gun to Brett.

Mosher yanked Melissa against his body and pressed the gun into the cold flesh at her temple. "Don't try anything foolish, Brett, or I'll blow your friend here away."

"Go ahead. Blow her away. She's nothing to me. Just another reporter."

Melissa swayed, her insides melting to nothingness. She sank against Mosher as her legs gave way beneath her. But not from fear. From the bitter knowledge that Brett meant exactly what he'd said. It was in the callous chill of his voice. In the casual sway of his stance. She was nothing to him.

Nothing.

The hurt rose up to choke her. She'd wanted love, but once more she'd made a miserable choice. Once more she'd found only heartbreak.

The gun pressed into her temple. Heartbreak and death.

"You're going to pay, Mosher. You're going to pay for Jason. And you're going to pay for Emily Sands."

"Emily? That wasn't my fault. She asked for it. All I wanted her to do was tell the police that you'd tried to strangle her. But the nosy loudmouth wouldn't cooperate. Instead she started nosing around in my files, collecting evidence about hospital fraud.''

Mosher tightened his grip on Melissa.

"I'm not going to jail. Not for the Sands woman. Not for Sylvia. Not for anybody.''

"Oh, you're going to jail, all right, Mosher. And you'll be there for a long, long time.''

"I'll take my chances, Samson. Now you just throw down your gun.'' He clicked off the safety and pushed the barrel harder against Melissa's temple. "Throw it down or she's history.''

"No way, Mosher. No way.''

The almost silent click of metal on metal seemed to explode in Melissa's ear. She collapsed against Mosher, falling silently to the ground.

"Damn you, Samson. Damn you to—''

Melissa heard the string of curses. But she hadn't heard a shot. Brett reached out his free hand and pulled her to him. He cradled her against his body, holding her like he'd never let her go.

"The gun wasn't loaded.'' Melissa said the words out loud though no one seemed to be listening. She tried to move, but Brett only held her tighter.

"You won't get away with this, Samson. You or your reporter friend.''

Melissa felt Brett's lips brush across the top of her head. The gun hadn't been loaded. She should have known, should have trusted the man she loved.

She leaned against his strong frame. Her rock. She'd deal with the truth about Mosher later. Right now all she could handle were feelings. Brett's arms around her felt wonderful.

"I'll call the police," Sylvia whispered, turning toward the house.

"That won't be necessary."

The voice was all too familiar. Melissa turned to see Marvin Brady and two uniformed policemen appear from the surrounding bushes.

"Good job, Samson. One of the nicest confessions I've ever heard. We could use you on all our cases."

"No, thanks. The wild creatures in Wyoming are a little more my style."

Melissa looked from Brett to Marvin, totally confused.

"We'll take it from here, Samson," Marvin announced, extending his hand to Brett. "You can take the lady home. It looks like you're her choice for the job."

Melissa didn't miss the touch of envy in Marvin's voice. But there was no arguing with his words. Brett was definitely her choice for the job.

BRETT TENDERLY LIFTED Melissa's foot, placing it atop the stack of fluffed pillows on the end of the sofa. "Now, don't move. I'll be right back with the ice pack and your cup of hot coffee."

"Okay, but hurry," Melissa urged. "I want to hear everything. You've made me wait long enough."

Brett bent over and placed a light kiss on her forehead. "Impatient, aren't you?"

Melissa slipped her hand behind his head and pulled it down, toward her waiting lips. She kissed him soundly, reveling in the feel of his strong, hard lips on hers, the taste of his salty maleness on her tongue.

Reluctantly, she pulled away. "Very impatient," she murmured softly, her voice low, breathy with desire.

"One more kiss like that, and you can forget any explanations tonight." He fluffed the pillows behind her head.

Melissa lay back contentedly. The cabin had never seemed as cozy as it did this minute. The logs in the fireplace cast a gentle glow as the yellow flames licked them into crackling submission. She pulled the flowered quilt tighter, letting its softness caress her toasty-warm skin.

The night had been a boiling pot of fervent emotions. She'd endured surprise, pain, fear, disgust, relief and heartbreak in a matter of minutes. Her body still trembled from the multitude of sensations that had coursed through her veins. But they all paled next to the glow of contentment she felt now.

Jason's murderer was behind bars. And so was his accomplice. Sylvia had not intentionally killed Jason, but she knew about the drugs Mosher had administered, and she was in on the plot to have his mental condition seriously questioned.

All for money.

She'd likely married Jason for his money, just as Brett had surmised. But that hadn't been enough. She'd wanted it all, her freedom and the wealth. And Mosher had been her way out. Only he'd had plans of his own.

Greed had provided Sylvia with riches for a while. Now it would reward her with a jail term.

Melissa listened to the noises coming from the kitchen—the clatter of spoons in pottery cups and the merry whistling of a Cajun tune Brett had learned from Cotile. Happiness filled her heart nearly to bursting.

Brett had been the perfect prince ever since they'd left the rose garden. He had taken her in his arms and carried her all the way to the car, not letting her place any weight on the throbbing ankle. He'd put her in the back seat and used their coats as a prop to keep the foot raised.

She'd blurted out everything about Beauregard's cross, about the dog's grave, about Sylvia ordering her off the place. Then she'd tried to ask a million questions, but Brett had insisted she rest. He'd promised to tell her everything as soon as they returned to the cabin. Everything about tonight.

And more.

But there was one thing she already knew for certain. It was time for her to learn to trust. She'd pushed Brett to the edge last night, forcing him to blurt out things that were far too personal, too painful to share just to satisfy someone's curiosity. All that to prove that he was worthy of her trust.

And tonight she'd jumped to conclusions again. She hadn't understood his actions, so she'd assumed the worst. She'd been willing to ignore everything she knew to be true about him in the face of circumstantial evidence. He'd looked and sounded like he didn't care if she lived or died, so as far as she was concerned, he didn't.

She was a smart and intuitive woman. She'd proved it more than once. But she could also be unbelievably stupid where love was concerned. She'd proved that, too.

In spite of all her mistakes, Brett had been there for her tonight. Holding her. Taking care of her. Loving her, though she wasn't sure he knew that yet.

She watched him as he crossed the room, balancing two cups of hot coffee and some fruit-laden sweet rolls on a wooden tray. He pulled a handmade cypress end table over so that Melissa could reach everything with a minimum of effort.

"Sit here, Brett." She raised up, making room for him next to her. Right where she wanted him.

He squeezed in and turned sideways, pulling her closer, wrapping her in the circle of his arms. He pulled off a bite of a sweet roll and fed it to her. "You need to keep your strength up. You're going to need it later. Now, what do you want to hear about first?"

"What made you decide to come to Samson Place tonight? Did you know I was there?"

"Not at first. I didn't get back here until after two. I waited at the airport until I got Eric's message that he was stuck in Wyoming in a blizzard. All the flights had been canceled until further notice. I drove here, but the note you'd left said you were going into New Orleans to answer Marvin's questions."

Brett broke off another piece of roll, putting part in his mouth and part in Melissa's. He let his fingers linger, tracing her bottom lip. He left her hungry for far more than the sweetness of the fruit.

"I didn't even suspect where you were until Brady showed up here at the house."

"I knew it. I didn't come in soon enough to suit him so he came looking for me."

"Not exactly." Brett sipped his coffee. "He came here to arrest me."

"Then he must have found out I'd lied about you."

"Yeah, with the help of a waitress at that greasy spoon where I met you."

"Where you kidnapped me," she corrected.

"Okay, if you want to get technical." His smile lit up his face and sent a warm glow deep into Melissa's body, heating places that would not be satisfied with mere smiles.

"He also talked to the manager of the motel where Mosher arranged to have your car ignited. They both described us to a *T.* Then there was the matter of some tranquilizers he'd found in the bedroom at the cabin."

Melissa cuddled closer in his arms. Yesterday she'd been concerned about the pills. Tonight they were unimportant. Trust made the difference.

"They were the pills I'd pretended to swallow when I was first admitted to Mosher's madhouse. I'd kept them with me. I figured they might come in handy when I finally got to talk to a judge."

"And I'm sure that was all Marvin needed."

"Right. Enough evidence to convince him his first instincts had been on target, that you were sheltering a dangerous escapee."

Brett trailed her neck with feathery kisses. "Only he didn't know how dangerous," he warned, his voice gravelly with desire.

"So you persuaded him to go to Samson Place with you?" Melissa was anxious for the explanations to continue. And to conclude. There were other, more delightful avenues to explore.

"And that turned out to be a monumental task. We had almost reached New Orleans before I could convince him you were there and possibly in deep trouble. Like everyone else, he was certain the eminent doctor and respectable heiress would pose no threat to a well-meaning reporter."

"Not unless you call murder a threat."

"So I told him. More than once. Finally, my hysterics got to him. I was out of my head with worry."

He whispered the words into her hair, while his hands caressed her, moving gently over her arms.

"I never want to know that kind of fear again—being unable to take care of you, not knowing if you're dead or alive." His voice broke, and he hugged her even tighter against his hard body. "I guess Brady figured it all out then. The way I felt about you and the truth of the danger. He speeded toward Samson Place, sirens blaring. We even picked up a couple more cops along the way."

Brett tilted Melissa's face so that he could look into her eyes. "He's a good cop. But there was a lot more to it than that. The man wanted you for himself." He planted a kiss on the tip of her nose. "But then, who wouldn't?"

Melissa ached for more of his lips, but there was still one little detail she hadn't quite figured out. "So that's why the gun wasn't loaded, Marvin had already removed the bullets."

"Not exactly. It was my gun. He'd taken it from me at the cabin, but he hadn't disarmed it. He tossed it to me just before I stuck it in Mosher's back."

"I'm surprised he left that chore to you."

"He didn't want to, believe me. But when we finally reached the garden and sized up the situation, Mosher's loaded gun was pointed right at you. I managed to talk Brady into letting me go in alone. It was me Mosher really wanted. I thought I could distract him long enough for you to get away."

"I still don't understand. If Marvin didn't take the bullets from the gun, why didn't it fire when Mosher pulled the trigger?"

"It was never loaded, Melissa, not since a few minutes after I took it from the glove compartment of old Carl's truck. I admit, I tried to buy some bullets once, when I thought I might need them to protect you, but the guy at the store asked too many questions. After that the infection took hold."

Melissa's head was still spinning from the night's excitement. It must be. Brett wasn't making sense.

"But at the truck stop, when you kidnapped me . . ."

"Not even then, Melissa. I was desperate. Desperate enough to kidnap a girl at gunpoint. But not at the point of a loaded gun. I was a shaking mess, coming off weeks of mind-killer drugs. I wasn't about to run around with a loaded gun. I might have killed someone."

"Just a reporter," she reminded him, only half teasing.

"An honest and very brave reporter," he whispered, burying his lips in her hair. "The woman I love. The woman I plan to marry."

Melissa turned her face to his, taking his lips with her own. This time there'd be no tempting, tantalizing sweetness. This time she wanted it all. She wanted passion, wild and unbridled. She wanted love and everything that went with it.

She wanted it tonight. Tomorrow. And forever.

And this time she could trust her heart completely. She'd fallen in love with the right man.

HARLEQUIN®

INTRIGUE®

WHO IS THIS

They say what makes a woman alluring is her air of mystery.
In August, Harlequin Intrigue brings you another very
mysterious woman—Joanna Wayne. We're proud to introduce
another new writer to Intrigue, as the
Woman of Mystery program continues.

And not only is the author a "Woman of Mystery"—
the heroine is, too!

Melissa Bentley is hiding—deep in the steamy bayou...from
an organization that wants her dead...and from a man who
has not only captured her heart, but who holds her captive....

Don't miss
#288 DEEP IN THE BAYOU by Joanna Wayne

Available in August 1994 wherever Harlequin books are sold.

Be on the lookout for more "Woman of Mystery" books in the
months to come, as we search out the best new writers, just
for you—only from Harlequin Intrigue!

HARLEQUIN INTRIGUE—NOT THE SAME OLD STORY!

WOMEN4

This summer, come cruising with Harlequin Books!

PORTS OF CALL

In July, August and September, excitement, danger and, of course, romance can be found in Lynn Leslie's exciting new miniseries PORTS OF CALL. Not only can you cruise the South Pacific, the Caribbean and the Nile, your journey will also take you to Harlequin Superromance®, Harlequin Intrigue® and Harlequin American Romance®.

- ♦ In July, cruise the South Pacific with SINGAPORE FLING, a Harlequin Superromance
- ♦ NIGHT OF THE NILE from Harlequin Intrigue will heat up your August
- ♦ September is the perfect month for CRUISIN' MR. DIAMOND from Harlequin American Romance

So, cruise through the summer with LYNN LESLIE and HARLEQUIN BOOKS!

CRUISE

HARLEQUIN®

I N T R I G U E®

As part of Harlequin Intrigue's "Decade of Danger and Desire," we invite you to

RETURN TO THE SCENE OF THE CRIME

Four of your favorite authors reprise the stories that *you* made some of the most popular Harlequin Intrigue titles over the past ten years. In these *brand-new* stories, you can pick up the loves and adventures of the characters you first met in the original novels...and delight in meeting some new ones.

In September, don't miss any of the
RETURN TO THE SCENE OF THE CRIME books:

TANGLED VOWS: *A 43 Light Street novel*
by Rebecca York
(based on SHATTERED VOWS, 1991)

WHO IS JANE WILLIAMS?
by M.J. Rodgers
(FOR LOVE OR MONEY, 1991)

CRIMSON NIGHTMARE
by Patricia Rosemoor
(CRIMSON HOLIDAY, 1988)

THE DREAMER'S KISS
by Laura Pender
(DÉJÀ VU, 1990)

Watch for details on how you can get the original novels on which these stories are based!

RETURN TO THE SCENE OF THE CRIME

RTSC

HARLEQUIN®

I N T R I G U E®

Ski through glitzy Aspen with the King of Rock 'n' Roll
for the hottest—yet most mysteriously chilling—
August of 1994 ever!

**#285
DON'T BE CRUEL
by Cassie Miles
August 1994**

Gina Robinson headed for glittering Aspen to purchase
her uncle's Elvis memorabilia...only to find herself
snowbound with Conner "Hound Dog" Hobarth. The two
built a cozy cabin fire destined to lead somewhere very
special. Unfortunately, the morning after, they found
Gina's uncle dead on the premises and discovered the law
thought the lovebirds had spent the night committing
murder!

ELVIS 94

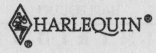

THE WEDDING GAMBLE
Muriel Jensen

Eternity, Massachusetts, was America's wedding town. Paul Bertrand knew this better than anyone—he never should have gotten soused at his friend's rowdy bachelor party. Next morning when he woke up, he found he'd somehow managed to say "I do"—to the woman he'd once jilted! And Christina Bowman had helped launch so many honeymoons, she knew just what to do on theirs!

THE WEDDING GAMBLE, available in September from American Romance, is the fourth book in Harlequin's new cross-line series, **WEDDINGS, INC.**

Be sure to look for the fifth book, **THE VENGEFUL GROOM,** by Sara Wood (Harlequin Presents #1692), coming in October.